THE DWARF

THE DWARF

by

PÄR LAGERKVIST

translated by
ALEXANDRA DICK

HILL AND WANG

New York

I AM twenty-six inches tall, shapely and well proportioned, my head perhaps a trifle too large. My hair is not black like the others', but reddish, very stiff and thick, drawn back from the temples and the broad but not especially lofty brow. My face is beardless, but otherwise just like that of other men. My eyebrows meet. My bodily strength is considerable, particularly if I am annoyed. When the wrestling match was arranged between Jehoshaphat and myself I forced him onto his back after twenty minutes and strangled him. Since then I have been the only dwarf at this court.

Most dwarfs are buffoons. They have to make jokes and play trick to make their masters and the guests laugh. I have never demeaned myself to anything like that. Nobody has even suggested that I should. My very appearance forbids such a use of me. My cast of countenance is unsuited to ridiculous pranks. And I never laugh. I am no buffoon. I am a dwarf and nothing but a dwarf.

On the other hand I have a sharp tongue which may occasionally give pleasure to some of those around me. That is not the same thing as being their buffoon.

I mentioned that my face was exactly like that of other men. That is not quite accurate, for it is very lined, covered with wrinkles. I do not look upon this as a blemish. I am made that way and I cannot help it if others are not. It shows me as I really am, unbeautified and undistorted. Maybe it was not meant to be like that, but that is exactly as I want to look.

The wrinkles make me look very old. I am not, but I have heard tell that we dwarfs are descended from a race older than that which now populates the world, and therefore we are old as soon as we are born. I do not know if this is true, but in that case we must be the original beings. I have nothing against belonging to a different race from the present one and showing it on my person.

I think that the others' faces are absolutely expressionless.

M Y MASTERS are very gracious to me, particularly the Prince, who is a great and powerful man, a man of great schemes, and one who knows how to put them into execution. He is a man of action, but at the same time a scholar who finds time for everything and likes to discuss all manner of subjects under heaven and on earth. He conceals his true aims by talking about something else.

It may seem unnecessary to be so preoccupied by everything (always supposing he really is), but perhaps it has to be, perhaps as a prince he is obliged to comprehend everything. He gives the impression of being able to understand and master anything, or at least of wishing to do so. Undeniably he is an imposing personality, the only one I have ever known whom I do not despise.

He is very treacherous.

I am well acquainted with my lord, but I do not profess to know him inside and out. His is a complicated nature which it is not easy to understand. It would be wrong to say that he is full of hidden riddles—not at all—but somehow or other he is difficult to know. I do not quite understand him myself, and I do not really know why I follow him with such doglike devotion. On the other hand he does not understand me either.

He does not impress me as he does the others, but I like to be in the service of a master who is so impressive. I will not deny that he is a great man; but nobody is great to his dwarf.

I follow him constantly, like a shadow.

PRINCESS Teodora is very dependent on me. I carry her secret in my heart. I have never breathed a word of it, and if they stretched me on the rack in the torture chamber with all its horrors, even than I should never betray anything. Why? I do not know. I hate her and I should like to see her dead, burning in the fires of hell with her legs astraddle and the flames licking her foul belly. I hate her lascivious mode of life, the lewd missives which she makes me carry to her lovers, her words of love which burn against my heart. But I betray nothing. I am always risking my life for her.

When she calls me into her chamber and whisperingly confides her messages to me, hiding the love letters under my jerkin, then I shiver all over and the blood rushes to my head. But she notices nothing, she never gives a thought to the fact that my life is at stake. Not her life, but mine! She merely smiles her scarcely perceptible, absent-minded smile, and lets me go on my dangerous mission. My share in her secret life counts as nothing with her. But she trusts me.

I hate all her lovers. I have wanted to fling myself upon every one of them and pierce them with my dagger to see their blood flow. Most of all I hate Don Riccardo; she has had him for several years now, and it looks as though she never intended to get rid of him. I find him repulsive.

Sometimes she lets me come into her chamber before she has risen, and exposes herself in all her shamelessness. She is no longer young, her breasts sag as she lies in the bed, playing with her jewels and taking them out of the casket proffered by her handmaid. I cannot understand how anyone can love her. She has nothing which a man could find desirable. One can only see that once upon a time she was utterly beautiful.

She asks me which jewels I think she should wear today. She likes asking me that. She lets them fall slowly between her narrow fingers and stretches herself indolently under the heavy silken coverlet. She is a whore. A whore in the bed of a magnificent prince. Her whole life is love which, like her jewels, she lets trickle through her fingers, while she lies smiling vaguely as she sees it run away between them.

At such moment she is often sad or pretends to be. With a wistful gesture she twines a gold chain around her neck and lets its great ruby glow between her breasts; then she asks if I think she ought to wear that chain. The scent of her around her bed makes me retch. I hate her, I want to see her burning in the fires of hell. But I answer that I think she ought to choose that particular one, and she sends me a grateful glance as though I had partaken of her grief and brought her rueful consolation.

[9]

Sometimes she calls me her only friend. Once she asked me if I loved her.

WHAT about the Prince? Does he suspect nothing? Or maybe everything?

It looks as though the matter of her secret life did not exist for him. But one cannot tell, with him one can never be quite sure of anything. He consorts with her in the daytime, and it seems as though he himself were daytime in person, for he is so utterly irradiated with the light of day. It is odd that such a person should be beyond my comprehension—just *he*! But perhaps that is because I am his dwarf, and again—he does not understand me either! I understand the Princess better than I do him, and that is not so remarkable, for after all I hate her. It is difficult to understand those whom one does not hate, for then one is unarmed, one has nothing with which to penetrate into their being.

What is his relationship to the Princess? Is he too her lover? Perhaps her only real lover? And is that why he seems to be so unmoved by all that she does elsewhere? I am upset—but not he?

I do not understand this impassive man. His superiority is something which irritates me unceasingly, causing me a discomfort of which I cannot be rid. I want him to be like me.

THE COURT is abuzz with strange people. Wise men who sit with their heads in their hands trying to discover the meaning of life; scholars who believe that they can follow the path of the stars with their aged bleary eyes, who even believe that the fate of mankind is mirrored up there in them. Gallows-birds and adventurers who read their languishing verses to the ladies of the court, and then are found spewing prone in the gutter at dawn (one was stabbed to death as he lay there, and I recall that another was thrashed because he had written a pasquinade against the Cavaliere Moroscelli). Loose-living artists who fill the churches with pious images; sculptors and draftsmen who are to build the new cathedral's campanile; dreamers and charlatans of every description. They come and go like the vagabonds they are, but some stay on for a long time as though they belonged here. All abuse the Prince's hospitality.

It is incomprehensible that he should want to have these futile people here, and still more incomprehensible that he should be able to sit and listen to them and their stupid chatter. I can understand that he may occasionally listen to poets reciting their verses; they can be regarded as buffoons such as are always kept at court. They laud the lofty purity of the human soul, great events and heroic feats, and there is nothing to be said against all that, particularly if their songs flatter him. Human beings need flattery; otherwise they do not fulfill their purpose, not even in their own eyes. And both the present and the past contain much that is beautiful and noble which, without due praise, would have been neither noble nor beautiful. Above all, they sing the praises of love, which is quite as it should be, for nothing else is in such need of transformation into something different. The ladies are filled with melancholy and their breasts heave with sighs; the men gaze vaguely and dreamily into space, for they all know what it is really like and realize that this must be an especially beautiful poem.

I also understand that there must be artists to paint religious pictures for the people, so that they may have something to worship which is not poor and dirty like themselves; beautiful, unearthly pictures of martyrs who, honored after execution, have been given costly garments and a gold ring around their pates, just as they too shall be honored after they have finished their miserable lives. Pictures which show the rabble that their God was crucified, and that it happened when He tried to do something here on earth, making them understand that there can be no hope down here. Those simple craftsmen are necessary to a prince, but I don't know what business they have here in the palace. They give the people somewhere to dwell, a temple, a prettily decked torture chamber to which they can retire at any time in order to find peace, a place where their God hangs always upon His cross. I understand that, for I am a Christian myself; I have been baptized into the same faith as they, and it is a valid baptism, though it was done as a joke at the wedding of Duke Gonzaga and Donna Elena, when I was carried into the castle chapel as their first born, to whom the bride had given birth on the wedding day to the astonishment of all present. I have often heard it related as a very good joke, and I remember that so it was, for I was eighteen years old when it happened, and the Prince had lent me for the ceremony.

But what I cannot grasp is how anybody can listen to the people who talk about the meaning of life, to the philosophers with their profound meditations over life and death and the eternal problems, to sophistical expositions of virtue and honor and chivalry. And to those who deceive themselves into thinking that they know something about the stars, and who believe that these stars have some connection with human destiny. They are blasphemers, though I do not know what it is they blaspheme; that has nothing to do with me. They are buffoons, though they do not know it, nor does anybody else. Nobody laughs at them, nobody gets the least pleasure out of their fancies, nobody has the faintest idea why they have been summoned here to court. But the Prince listens to them as though their words were pregnant with meaning, and meditatively strokes his beard while he lets me fill their goblets, which are of silver like his own. The only time anybody ever laughs during their sessions is when they lift me onto their knees in order to help me pour the wine.

Who knows anything about the stars? Who can read their secret? Can these men? They believe that they can commune with the universe, and rejoice when they receive sapient replies. They spread out their star-maps and read the heavens like a book. But they are the authors of the book, and the stars continue on their shadowy ways and have no inkling of its contents.

I too read in the book of the night, but I cannot interpret it. My wisdom shows me not only the writing, but also that it cannot be interpreted.

At night they sit in their tower, the western tower, with their tubes and their quadrants, and believe that they are consorting with the universe. And I sit in the tower opposite which houses the old dwarfs' apartment, where I live alone since I throttled Jehoshaphat, under the low ceilings suitable to our tribe, with windows small as arrow slits. Once upon a time many dwarfs dwelt here, collected from distant lands, even from the kingdom of the Moors, the gifts of princes and popes and cardinals, or goods of exchange, as is our custom. We dwarfs have no homeland, no parents; we allow ourselves to be born of strangers, anywhere, in secret, among the poorest and most wretched, so that our race should not die out. And when these stranger parents discover that they have begotten a creature of our tribe they sell us to powerful princes that we may amuse them with our misshapen bodies and be their jesters. Thus did my mother sell me, turning away from me in disgust when she saw what she had borne, and not understanding that I was of an ancient race. She was paid twenty scudi for me and with them she bought three cubits of cloth and a watchdog for her sheep.

I sit at the dwarfs' window and gaze out into the night, exploring it as they do. I need no tubes nor telescopes, for my gaze itself is deep enough. I too read in the book of the night.

THERE is an explanation for the Prince's interest in all these scholars, artists, philosophers, and stargazers, and it is a very simple one. He wants his court to be renowned and famous, and himself as honored and illustrious as possible. He wants to attain something which everyone can understand and which, as far as I know, is coveted by all mankind.

I thoroughly understand and approve.

The Condottiere Boccarossa has arrived in the town and installed himself and his great train in the Palazzo Geraldi, which has been uninhabited since that family's exile. He visited the Prince and remained for several hours. Nobody else was permitted to be present.

He is a great and celebrated condottiere.

Work on the campanile has begun and we have been to see how far they have progressed. It will tower high above the dome of the cathedral, and when once the bells ring they will echo up to heaven. That is a pretty thought, as thoughts should be. The bells will hang higher than any others in Italy.

The Prince is much preoccupied with this building and this is quite understandable. He studied the drawings again and again on the spot, and he was entranced by the reliefs depicting scenes from the life of the Crucified One with which the base of the campanile is being decorated. So far they have not progressed much beyond this point.

It may never be completed. Many of my lord's building ventures are never completed. They stand there, half-finished, beautiful as the ruins of some great conception. But ruins are also memorials to their creator, and I have never denied that he is a great prince. When he walks through the streets I have no objection to walking by his side. Everybody looks up to him, nobody sees me. Nor are they meant to. They salute him respectfully as though they felt him to be a superior being, but that is because they are a pack of ingratiating cowards, not because they love or esteem him, as he believes. If I walk alone in the town they see me at once and fling taunts after me. "That's his dwarf! If you kick him, you kick his master!" They do not dare do that, but they throw dead rats and other foulnesses from the muck-heaps at me. When I draw my sword in rage, they roar with laughter. "What a mighty lord we have!" they shout. I cannot defend myself, for we do not fight with the same weapons. I have to run away with my clothing all soiled and dirty.

A dwarf always knows more about everything than his master.

I N POINT of fact I do not mind enduring that for the sake of my Prince. It proves that I am a part of him and occasionally represent his noble person. Even the ignorant mob understands that the master's dwarf is really the master himself, just as the castle is he with its towers and battlements, and the court with all its pomp and splendor, and the executioner who sends the heads rolling on the square outside, and the treasury with its measureless wealth, and the castellan who doles out bread to the poor in time of famine—all that is *He*. They have no notion of the power which I really represent. And it fills me with satisfaction to see that I am hated!

I dress myself as much as possible like the Prince, the same cut and the same materials. Any pieces left over from a suit of his ordering are used for me. At my side I carry a sword as he does, only shorter. And if anybody pays heed to my deportment, it is as dignified as his.

Thus I have become rather like the Prince, only a great deal smaller. If anyone looked at me through the kind of glass with which the buffoons in the western tower study the stars, they might think that I was he.

There is a great difference between dwarfs and children. Because they are about the same size, people think that they are alike, and that they suit each other; but they do not. Dwarfs are set to play with children, forced to do so, without a thought being given to the fact that a dwarf is the opposite to a child and that he is born old. As far as I know, dwarf children never play—why should they? It would only look macabre, with their wizened old faces. It is nothing less than torture to use us dwarfs like that. But human beings know nothing about us.

My masters have never forced me to play with

Angelica, but she herself has done so. I won't say that she did it out of spite, but when I look back on that time, especially when she was quite tiny, it seems as though I had been the victim of carefully thought-out malice. That infant, whom some people think so wonderful with her round blue eyes and her little pursed mouth, has tormented me almost more than anyone else at court. Every morning, from the time she could scarcely toddle, she would come staggering into the dwarf's apartment with her kitten under her arm. "Piccoline, will you play with us?" I answer: "I cannot, I have more important things to think about, my day is not meant for play." "Then what are you going to do?" she asks impertinently. "One cannot explain that to a child," I reply. "But at least you're going out, you aren't going to lie abed all day! I've been up such a long long time!" And I have to go out with her, I dare not refuse for fear of my masters, though inside I am raging with fury. She takes my hand as though I were her playmate; she is always wanting to hold my hand, though there is nothing I detest so much as sticky childish paws. I clench my fist in wrath, but she simply takes hold of my fist instead and drags me around everywhere, chattering all the time. We visit her dolls which have to be fed and dressed, the puppies sprawling half-blind outside the kennel, the rose garden where we have to play with the kitten.

She takes a tiresome interest in all kinds of animals, not full-grown ones, but their young—in fact, in everything small. She can sit and play with her kitten for ages and expect me to join in. She believes that I too am a child with a child's delight in everything. I! I delight in nothing.

Sometimes it really seems as though a sensible idea were passing through her head when she notices how bored and bitter I am, for she looks surprisedly up at my furrowed old man's face. "Why don't you enjoy playing?"

And when she receives no answer from my compressed lips or from my cold dwarf's eyes with the centuries of experience in their depths, a shyness shadows her newborn baby eyes, and she is actually silent for a while.

What is play? A meaningless dabbling with nothing at all. A strange "let's pretend" way of dealing with things. They must not be treated as they really are, not seriously; one is only pretending. Astrologers play with the stars, the Prince plays with his building, his churches, the crucifixion scenes, and the campaniles, Angelica with her dolls—they all play, all pretend something. Only I despise this pretending. Only I *am*.

Once I crept into her room as she lay sleeping with her detestable kitten beside her in bed and cut off its head with my dagger. Then I threw it out onto the dungheap beneath the castle window.

I was so furious that I hardly knew what I was doing. That is to say, I knew only too well. I was carrying out a plan which had long been germinating during those revolting playtimes in the rose garden. She was inconsolable when she saw that it was gone, and when everybody said that of course it must be dead, she sickened with an unknown fever and was ill for a long time, so that I, thank goodness, did not have to see her. When at last she got up again, I was obliged to listen all the more to her woeful narrative of her darling's fate, of the incredible thing which had happened. Nobody cared how the cat had disappeared, but the whole court had been upset because of some inexplicable drops of blood on the girl's neck, which could be interpreted as an evil omen. Anything which can possibly be taken as an omen is of tremendous interest to them.

In fact, throughout her childhood she never left me in peace although the games gradually changed. She was always hanging on to me and would have liked to confide in me, though I did not want her confidences. Sometimes I wonder if her importunate affection for me might not have had the same source as her weakness for kittens, puppies, ducklings, and so on; if, maybe, she were not happy in the grownup world, perhaps feared it, after some scare or other. It had nothing to do with me! It was no doing of mine if she wandered about in loneliness. But she always wanted to cling to me and this did not lessen after she had left her infancy behind her. Her mother ceased caring about her as soon as she stopped being doll-like. She was pretending too, everybody pretends. And her father, of course, had his own business to attend to. He may have had other reasons for not being interested in her, but that is a matter on which I will not give my opinion.

Not until she was ten or twelve did she begin to be silent and self-contained, and I was rid of her at last. Since then she has left me in peace, thank goodness, and keeps to herself. But I still fume when I think how much I have had to endure for her sake.

Now she is beginning to grow up, she is fifteen and will soon be reckoned a woman. But she is still very childish and does not conduct herself at all like a lady of quality. It is impossible to guess who is her father. It might be the Prince, but she may just as well be a bastard, and this treatment of her as though she were a princess may be quite superfluous. Some call her beautiful. I can see nothing beautiful in the childish face with its half-open mouth and big blue eyes which look as if they understand nothing at all.

Love is something which dies and when dead it rots and becomes soil for a new love. Then the dead love continues its secret life in the living one, and thus in reality there is no death in love.

As far as I can understand this is the experience of the Princess, and on it she bases her happiness. For undoubtedly she is happy; she spreads happiness around her in her own way. For the moment Don Riccardo is happy.

The Prince also, perhaps for the feeling which he once kindled in her, is still alive. He pretends that her love still lives. They both pretend that their love still lives.

Once the Princess had one of her lovers tortured, because he had betrayed her. The Prince suspected nothing, and she induced him to condemn the other for a crime which he had never committed. I was the only one who knew the true circumstances, and I was present during the torture in order to let her know how he bore it. He was not in the least heroic—about average.

Maybe he is the girl's father. How should I know?

It might just as well be the Prince, for the Princess cajoled him most endearingly, and at that time their love had a second blooming. She embraced him every night, offering him her betrayed bosom which hungered for its lost lover. She caressed her Prince as though he were a man who should be tortured, and he returned her caresses as in their first passionate nights of love. The dead love continued its secret life in the living one.

THE PRINCESS' confessor comes every Saturday morning at the same time. By then she is up and fully dressed and has knelt in prayer for two hours before the crucifix. She is well prepared for her confession.

She has nothing to confess, but not because she lies or dissimulates. On the contrary, she always speaks freely from the fullness of her heart. She has no conception of sin. She does not know that she has done anything wrong, except perhaps been a little violent with her handmaid when her coiffure was fumbled. She is like an unwritten page and the confessor bends smiling over her as though she were an unspotted virgin.

Her eyes are brilliant and candid after her prayers and her submersion in the world of the crucifix. The tortured little man on his toy cross has suffered for her sake, and all guilt, even the memory of it, has been erased from her soul. She feels strong and rejuvenated and at the same time in a mood of dreamy piety and self-communion which suits her serious unpainted face and simple black gown. She seats herself and writes to her lover, telling him how she feels, a gentle sisterly letter without mention of love or rendezvous.

When she feels like this she cannot endure the slightest approach to frivolity. I have to take the letter to the lover.

There can be no doubt that she is profoundly religious. To her, religion is something essential, something absolutely real. She needs it and she uses it. It is part of her heart and soul.

Is the Prince religious too? That is more difficult to say. Of course he is, in his own way, for he is everything, *everything* is within his range—but can that be called religious? He likes to think that such a thing exists, he likes listening to talk about it, to eloquent and learned discussions about its world of ideas—but how could anything in humanity be alien to him? He likes triptychs and madonnas painted by famous artists, and fine handsome temples, particularly those he has built himself. I do not know if that is religion. It is quite possible. And as a prince he is of course as genuinely religious as she. He understands that the religious hunger of the people must be satisfied, and his door is always open for those who do so. Priests and all kinds of spiritual persons are familiars here. But is he, like her, religious in himself? That is something quite different, and I do not intend to give any opinion on it.

But again, there can be no doubt that she is deeply religious.

[25]

Perhaps, in their own way, they are both religious.

WHAT IS religion? I have given much thought to it, but in vain.

I pondered it especially that time a few years ago when I was compelled to officiate as a bishop in full canonicals at the carnival and give holy communion to the dwarfs of the Mantua court whom their Prince had brought here for the festival. We met at a miniature sanctuary which had been set up in one of the castle halls, and around us sat all the sniggering guests: knights and nobles and young coxcombs in their absurd apparel. I raised the crucifix and all the dwarfs fell on their knees. "Here is your savior," I declared in a sonorous voice, my eyes flaming with passion. "Here is the savior of all the dwarfs, himself a dwarf, who suffered under the great prince Pontius Pilate, and was nailed to his little toy cross for the joy and ease of all men." I took the chalice and held it up to them. "This is his dwarf's blood, in which all iniquities are cleansed and all dirty souls become as white as snow." Then I took the host and showed it to them and ate and drank of both in their sight, as is the custom, while I expounded the holy mysteries. "I eat his body which was deformed like yours. It tastes as bitter as gall, for it is full of hatred. May you all eat of it. I drink his blood, and it burns like a fire which cannot be quenched. It is as though I drink my own.

"Savior of all the dwarfs, may thy fire consume the whole world!"

And I threw the wine out over those who sat there, staring in gloom and amazement at our somber communion feast.

I am no blasphemer. It was they who blasphemed, not I, but the Prince had me clapped in irons for several days. The little jest had been intended to amuse, but I had spoiled it all and the guests had been very upset, almost scared. There were no chains small enough so they had to be specially made, and the smith thought that it was a great deal of trouble for such a short sentence. But the Prince said that it might be as well to have them for another time. He let me go sooner than had been planned, and I rather think he punished me merely for the sake of the guests, for as soon as they had left I was released. During the time that followed, however, he looked at me rather askance and did not seem to want to be alone with me; it was almost as though he were somewhat afraid of me.

Of course the dwarfs understood nothing. They scuttled around like frightened hens and squeaked with their miserable castrato voices. I don't know where they get those ridiculous voices; my own is rich and deep. But they are cowed and castrated to the depths of their souls, and most of them are buffoons who shame their race by their gross jests about their own bodies.

They are a contemptible clan. So that I need not see them, I have made the Prince sell all the dwarfs here, one after the other, until I am the only one at the court. I am glad they are gone and the dwarfs' apartment is empty and deserted when I sit there at night with my meditations. I am glad that Jehoshaphat is gone too, so that I am quit of his crumpled old woman's face and his piping voice. I am glad to be *alone*.

It is my fate that I hate my own people. My race is detestable to me.

But I hate myself too. I eat my own splenetic flesh. I drink my own poisoned blood. Every day I perform my solitary communion as the grim high priest of my people.

AFTER THIS incident which caused so much offense, the Princess began to behave in a rather peculiar way. On the morning of my liberation she called me in to her, and when I entered the bedchamber she looked at me in silence with a thoughtful searching gaze. I had expected reproaches, perhaps more punishment, but when at last she spoke she admitted that my communion service had made a deep impression on her, that there had been something dark and terrible about it which had appealed to something within her. How had I been able to penetrate to her secret depths like that and speak to them?

I did not understand. I seized the opportunity to sneer as she lay there in the bed gazing vaguely past me.

She asked what I thought it felt like to hang on a cross. To be scourged, tortured, to die? And she said that she realized Christ must hate her, that He must be full of hatred while suffering for her sake.

I did not bother to reply, nor did she continue the conversation, but lay staring into space with dreaming eyes.

Then she dismissed me with a gesture of her beautiful hand and called to her tirewoman to fetch her crimson gown because she was going to get up.

I still don't understand what possessed her just then.

I HAVE noticed that sometimes I frighten people; what they really fear is themselves. They think it is I who scare them, but it is the dwarf within them, the ape-faced manlike being who sticks up its head from the depths of their souls. They are afraid because they do not know that they have another being inside them. They are scared when anything rises to the surface, from their inside, out of some of the cesspools in their souls, something which they do not recognize and which is not a part of their real life. When nothing is visible above the surface, they are utterly fearless. They go about, tall and unconcerned, with their smooth faces which express nothing at all. But inside them is always something else which they ignore and, without knowing it, they are constantly living many kinds of lives. They are so strangely secretive and incoherent.

And they are deformed though it does not show on the outside. I live only my dwarf life. I never go around tall and smooth-featured. I am ever myself, always the same, I live *one* life alone. I have no other being inside me. And I recognize everything within me, nothing ever comes up from my inner depths, nothing there is shrouded in mystery. Therefore I do not fear the things which frighten them, the incoherent, the unknown, the mysterious. Such things do not exist for me. There is nothing "different" about me.

Fear? What is it? Is it what I feel when I lie alone in the dwarfs' apartment at night and see the ghost of Jehoshaphat nearing my bed, when he comes to me, deathly pale with blue marks around his neck and gaping mouth?

I feel no anguish and no regret, I am not unduly disturbed. When I see him I merely think that he is dead and that since his death I have been completely alone.

I want to be alone. I don't want there to be anybody else except me. And I can see that he is dead. It is only his ghost, and I am absolutely alone in the dark as I have been ever since I strangled him.

There is nothing frightening in that.

A TALL man has come to the court and the Prince treats him with peculiar courtesy, almost with reverence. He has been invited here, and the Prince says that he has long awaited him, and now is very happy that the visit has been vouchsafed to him at last. He consorts with him as though he were an equal.

Everybody does not find this ridiculous, some say that he really is a great man and the equal of a prince. But he does not dress like a prince, his clothes are very simple. I have not yet discovered what he is and why he should be so remarkable, but in due course I shall do so. They say he is going to stay here for a long time.

I will not deny that there is something imposing about him. His bearing is more naturally dignified than most, his brow is lofty and what men generally call thoughtful, and his face with its grizzled beard is noble and quite handsome. There is something distinguished and harmonious about him and his aspect is full of calm and dignity.

In what way is he misshapen, I wonder?

THE NOTABLE guest eats at the Prince's table. All the time they discourse on the most varied topics, and while serving my lord as is his wish, I can hear that he is a man of education. His knowledge seems to embrace everything and everything seems to interest him. He tries to explain it all but, in contrast to the others, he is not always convinced that his explanations are correct. After a long and exhaustive exposition of some problem or other, he can sit silent and pensive, and then make the reflection: "But perhaps it is not thus." I don't know what to make of that. It can be termed a kind of wisdom, but it may also mean that he does not really know anything for certain, and that the laboriously constructed train of reasoning is therefore devoid of meaning. And my experience with human thought leads me to believe that this may be the case. There are not many who understand that this can give cause for modesty. It is possible that he does.

However, the Prince pays no attention to such things, but listens as though he were sitting by a clear spring bubbling with knowledge and wisdom. He hangs on his words like a humble student listening to his master, although at the same time he naturally retains his princely dignity. Sometimes he calls him "Great Master." Then I wonder what can be the reason for all this ingratiating humility. With my master there is always a reason. Generally the scholar pretends not to hear this obsequious address. It is possible that he really is unpretentious, but on the other hand he sometimes expresses himself with great decisiveness, giving his opinion with clarity and conviction and exposing his reasons with an intelligence which seems both sharp and penetrating. He does not always vacillate.

His voice is always calm, rich and unusually clear. He is friendly to me and appears to take an interest in me. Why, I do not know. Sometimes he almost reminds me of the Prince, though I cannot explain quite how.

He is not treacherous.

THE REMARKABLE stranger has begun his preparations for a painting on the wall of the refectory of the Franciscan monastery of Santa

Croce. So he is nothing more than a manufacturer of holy pictures and the like, the same as all the others here. That was all his "remarkableness."

But it does not follow that he is merely comparable with his simple fellow craftsmen, that he may not also be something more than that. One must admit that he is more impressive than they, and it is understandable that the Prince should listen most to him; but that he should hearken to him night and day as though he were an oracle, and let him eat at his table—for that I can find no explanation. After all, he is nothing more than a professional craftsman; what he does is achieved by his own hands, even if his culture and imagination include so much—too much for him to understand! I do not know how skilled his hands are. I hope they know their trade, since the Prince has engaged him, but he himself confesses that his imagination involves him in tasks beyond its compass. He must be a visionary standing on shifting sands despite all his brilliance and ingenuity, and the world which he pretends to create must be a mirage.

But oddly enough I have not yet formed any definite opinion about him; why, I do not know. As a rule I have a very clear opinion of those with whom I am faced. Apparently his personality, like his figure, towers above the common run of men, but I do not know the secret of his superiority, or if he really is so superior. He must resemble the other people whom I have met.

Anyhow I am convinced that the Prince has an exaggerated notion of his value.

He is called Bernardo, a very ordinary name.

HE DOES not interest the Princess; after all he is an old man, and the conversation of men with each other seems unfamiliar to her. When she is present during their lengthy discussions she sits silent and remote. I don't believe she even hears what the remarkable man is saying.

But he appears to be very much interested in her. He observes her in secret, unnoticed by the others. I have seen him. He seems to study her face with a pensive gaze which becomes more and more contemplative, as though seeking something there. What can there be about her which fascinates him so?

Her face is not at all interesting. It is easy to see that she is a harlot, though she hides it beneath a smooth deceitful surface. It does not need much observation to realize that. And then what is there left to study and seek after in her lascivious face? What fascination does it hold?

But he is obviously fascinated by everything. I have seen him pick up a stone from the ground and examine it with the deepest interest, turn and twist it, and finally pocket it, as though it were a rarity. Anything and everything seems to fascinate him. Is he a lunatic?

An enviable lunatic! One for whom a pebble has value must be surrounded by treasures wherever he goes.

He is incredibly curious. He ferrets about everywhere, wanting to know the why and wherefore of everything. He asks the workmen about their tools and their way of working, and criticizes and corrects them. He comes back from his wanderings outside the town with bunches of flowers and sits down and pulls them to bits to see what they look like inside. And he can stand for hours watching the flight of the birds, as though that too were something extraordinary. He can even stare at the impaled heads of murderers and thieves outside the castle gate (they are so old that nobody else bothers to spare them a glance) as though they were strange riddles, and he sketches them in silverpoint. And a few days ago when Francesco was hanged on the square outside, he stood in the crowd right at the front among the children, the better to see everything. At night he stands and stares at the stars. His curiosity knows no bounds.

Can it really be that anything and everything is of interest?

I DON'T give a fig for his pokings and fer-retings, but if he touches me again I shall give him a taste of my dagger! My mind is made up, whatever the cost!

Tonight when I was pouring his wine he took my hand and wanted to look at it, but I drew it back in anger. But the Prince smiled and said that I must show it to him. He studied it closely, with shameless impertinence, scrutinized the knuckles and the wrinkles around the wrist, and even tried to push up my sleeve so as to see my arm. I pulled it back again in my anger, for I was seething with fury. They both smiled as I stood there with flaming eyes.

If he touches me once more, I shall have his blood!

I cannot bear being touched by anyone, I cannot tolerate any kind of offense against my body.

There is a queer rumor going around that he has persuaded the Prince to give him Francesco's body in order to cut it up and see what a human inside looks like. It cannot be true. It is too incredible. And they cannot possibly have taken down the body, for it is supposed to hang there as a warning to the people, and to shame the criminal. Thus ran the sentence and why should not this scoundrel be pecked to pieces by the crows as much as the others? I had the misfortune to be acquainted with him and know only too well that he deserved the extremest punishment. Many a time has he taunted me in the streets. If they take him down it will not be quite the same punishment as the other gallows-birds'.

I heard it first this evening. It is night now, so I cannot see if the corpse is still hanging out there.

I cannot believe that it is true, that the Prince could give his consent to such a thing!

IT IS true! The rascal is no longer on the gallows! And I have also discovered where he is; I surprised the sage in the middle of his nefarious handiwork!

I had noticed that there was something going on in the cellar, for a door which is generally closed was open there. I noticed that yesterday, though I did not give it a second thought. Today I went there to investigate and found the door still ajar. I entered a long dark passage and came to another door, which was not shut either, and I slipped noiselessly in. There in a large room stood the old man in the light of a narrow slit in the southern wall, bending over Francesco's cloven body! At first I could not believe my eyes, but there it lay opened up, with the entrails visible, and the heart and the lungs, looking like an animal. I have never seen anything so disgusting, I could never even conceive of anything so revolting as the inside of a human being. But he stood bent over it, studying it with tense interest, while he carefully cut around the region of the heart with a slender knife. He was so fascinated by what he was doing that he did not even notice I was in the room. Nothing else seemed to exist for him except his nauseating occupation. But at last he raised his head and looked up with a contented gleam in his eyes. His face was as delighted as though he were at a festival. I could look at him as much as I wanted, for he was standing in the light whereas I was in the deep shadow. Besides, he was completely entranced as though he were a prophet communing with God. It really was repellent.

The peer of princes! A prince who busies himself interpreting conundrums in the bowels of a criminal, who burrows into corpses!

TONIGHT they sat up until after midnight and talked and talked as never before. They worked themselves up into an ecstasy with their talk. They spoke of nature, of its inexhaustible greatness and riches. One great continuity, a single miracle! The veins which lead the blood around in the body as the spring water is led around in the earth; lungs which breathe as the oceans breathe

with their ebb and flow; the skeleton which sup-
ports the body as the stones support the earth and
the soil which is its flesh; the fire within the earth
which is like the warmth of the soul and which
also has come from the sun, the sacred sun which
was worshiped of yore and from which all souls
originate, which is the source of all life and which
illumines the heavenly bodies of the universe with
its light. For our world is only one among the innumerable stars of the universe.

They were as though possessed, and I had to
listen to them, regardless of what they said, without being able to protest. I am more and more
convinced that he is a lunatic and on the way to
making my Prince one too. It is incredible that my
lord should be so weak and malleable in his hands.

How can anyone seriously believe in such fan-
tasies? How can anybody believe in the continuity,
the divine harmony in everything, as he also called
it? How can anybody use such fine-sounding,
meaningless words? Miracles of nature! I thought
of Francesco's guts and nearly vomited.

What bliss to behold the wonderful riches of nature, they exclaimed. There is so much to be explored. And man shall become rich and powerful
by learning to know all that, all these secret forces,
and how to make use of them. The elements shall
bow before his will; fire shall serve him in humility, its turbulence held in curb; the earth shall bear

fruit a hundredfold, because he has discovered the laws of fertility, the rivers shall be his obedient chained slaves, and the oceans shall carry his ships around the wide world which floats in space like a wonderful star. Even the air shall be subdued, for some day he will learn to imitate the flight of the birds and, buoyant as they, glide with them and the stars toward goals which no human thought can encompass.

Ah, life is wonderful and human existence unfathomable in its greatness!

There was no end to their jubilation. They were like children dreaming of toys, so many toys that they did not know what to do with them all. I looked at them with my dwarf's eyes without moving a muscle of my ancient furrowed face. Dwarfs are not like children; they never play. I reached up to fill their beakers as they emptied them in the course of their garrulous speech.

What do they know of the greatness of life? How do they know it is great? It is only a phrase, something they enjoy saying. One might just as well affirm that it was small, insignificant, completely unimportant, an insect that one can crush on a fingernail. And one might add that it has no objection to being crushed on a fingernail, being just as contented with its end as with anything else. And why should it not be so? Why should it be so anxious to exist? Why should it strive for existence or for anything else either? Why should it not be completely indifferent to everything?

Look into the heart of nature? What pleasure can there be in that? And if they really could do such a thing it would fill them with terror. They think that like everything else it is made for them, for their well-being and their happiness, so that their life shall be great and wonderful. What do they know about it? How do they know that any heed is paid to them and their strange childish desires?

They think that they can read in the book of nature, that it is lying open before them. They even believe that they can look on ahead in the book and read the blank pages where nothing is written. Heedless, conceited lunatics! There is no limit to their shameless self-sufficiency!

Who knows what nature carries in her womb? Who can even guess at it? Does a mother know what she has conceived? How could she? She bides her time, and eventually we see the thing to which she has given birth. A dwarf could tell them about that.

He diffident! There I was wrong. On the contrary, he is the most arrogant person I have ever met. His whole spirit and being breathe arrogance. And his mind is so presumptuous that it would fain lord it like a prince over a world which it does not own.

He may appear diffident when he sets himself to investigating all manner of things, saying he does not know this or that, but is trying to resolve them to the best of his ability. But he thinks that he knows the end and aim of everything, and the reason why! His humility applies to the small things only, not to the great. It is a strange kind of diffidence.

Everything has a meaning of its own, all that happens and preoccupies mankind. But life itself can have no meaning. Otherwise it would not be.

Such is *my* belief.

O SHAME! O dishonor! Never have I endured such degradation as that which was inflicted on me that terrible day. I shall try to write down what happened, though I would rather not remind myself of it.

The Prince had commanded me to seek out Maestro Bernardo who was working in the refectory at Santa Croce, saying he had need of me. I went there, though I was annoyed at being treated as though I were the servant of this haughty man who is no concern of mine. He received me in the friendliest fashion and said that he had always been greatly interested in dwarfs. I wondered: "What has not interested this man who wants to know all about Francesco's intestines and the stars of heaven? But," I continued to myself, "he knows nothing of me, the dwarf." After further amiable empty words he said that he wished to make a picture of me. At first I thought he meant my portrait, which the Prince perchance had bespoken, and I could not help feeling flattered. Nevertheless I replied that I did not wish to have my likeness reproduced. "Why not?" he asked. I answered, as was only natural: "I wish to possess my own face." He thought this strange, smiled somewhat, but then admitted that there was something in what I said. But, even when unreproduced, one's face is the property of many, in fact of all who look upon it. And here it was a question of a drawing of me which should show my shape, and therefore I must take off my clothes so that he could make a sketch of my body. I felt myself grow livid with wrath or fear (I know not which prevailed), and they both shook me so that I trembled all over.

He noted the violent agitation which his outrageousness aroused in me and began to say that there was no shame in being a dwarf and showing it. He always felt the same deep reverence for nature, even when its caprice created something out of the ordinary. There is never any disgrace in showing oneself as one is to another person, and nobody really possesses himself.

"But I do," I cried, beside myself with passion. "You don't possess yourselves, but I do!"

He listened to my outburst with perfect calm, he even observed it with a curious interest which agitated me still more. Then he said that he must begin—and drew nearer to me. "I can't bear any offense against my body!" I shrieked wildly, but he took not the slightest notice, and when he realized that I would never strip of my own free will, he prepared to undress me himself. I managed to jerk my dagger from its sheath and he seemed very surprised to see it gleaming in my hand. He took it away from me and laid it carefully down a little distance away. "I believe you are dangerous," he said, looking thoughtfully at me. I felt myself sneer at this remark. Then, placid as ever, he began to take off my clothes and exposed my body most shamelessly. I resisted desperately, fought with him as for my life, but all in vain, for he was stronger than I. When he had completed his vile task he lifted me onto a scaffold in the middle of the room.

I stood there defenseless, naked, incapable of action, though I was foaming with rage. And he stood some distance away from me, quite unmoved, and examined me, scrutinizing my shame with a cold and merciless gaze. I was utterly exposed to that outrageous gaze which explored and assimilated me as though I were his property. Having to stand like that and submit to somebody else's scrutiny was such a degradation that I still burn with shame to think that I ever was forced to endure it. I still recall the sound of his silverpoint as it glided over the paper, perhaps the same silverpoint with which he had limned the dried heads outside the castle gates, and all the other abominations. His glance remained unchanged, sharp as a dagger tip, and it seemed to pierce through me.

I have never hated the human race so much as during that ghastly hour. My hatred was so alive that I almost thought I should lose consciousness, everything went black before my eyes. Is there anything more vile than these beings, anything more detestable?

On the opposite wall I could see his great painting, which is supposed to be such a masterpiece. At that time it was still in its initial stages, but it seemed to represent the Last Supper, with Christ and His disciples at their love feast. I glared at them, sitting there with their pure solemn faces, believing that they were exalted above all others, grouped around their heavenly Lord, the one with the celestial light around His head. I rejoiced to think that soon He would be taken, that Judas, sitting huddled in his far corner, would soon betray Him. I thought: "Now He is still loved and honored, now He still sits at His feast—while I stand here in my shame! But His shame is on its way! Soon He will no longer be sitting there with

His followers, but hanging alone on a cross, betrayed by them. He will hang there as naked as I
am now, as humiliated as I, exposed to the stares
of all, mocked and defiled. And why not? Why
should He not suffer the same ignominy as I? He
has always been encompassed with love, nourished
Himself on love—while I have been nourished on
hate. From my birth I have sucked the bitter juice
of hate, I have lain at a breast filled with gall,
while He was suckled by the mild and gracious
Madonna and drank the sweetest mother's milk
that ever was. He sits there all innocent and kind
and cannot believe that anyone should hate Him
or want to harm Him. Why not? Why not He?
He believes that everybody on earth must love
Him because He was begotten by his heavenly
Father. What simplicity! What childish igno-
rance! That is just why they cherish their secret
rancor toward Him, just because of that miracle.
Mankind does not like to be violated by God."

I looked at Him again when at last I had been
liberated from my unspeakable humiliation and
stood at the door of that diabolical room where I
had undergone my deepest degradation. I thought:
"Soon You are going to be sold for a few scudi to
the noble, high-minded people, You as well as I!"

And in my wrath I slammed the door on Him
and His great master Bernardo, who was standing
sunk in contemplation before his exalted work,

already oblivious of me, who, through him, had suffered such agony.

I WOULD rather not recall what happened in Santa Croce, I should like to forget it, but I cannot help thinking about it. While I was dressing I could not avoid seeing some sketches which were strewn about, representing the oddest creatures, monsters such as never have been seen and which do not exist. They were something between men and beasts, women with bats' wings between their long hairy fingers, men with lizards' faces and legs and bodies like toads; others flying about like devils with cruel vulture faces and spread claws instead of hands, and beings which were neither men nor women, resembling sea monsters with twining tentacles and cold wicked human eyes. I was astounded by all these frightful monstrosities and I cannot rid myself of them yet; I still see them before me. How can his imagination dwell upon such things? Why does he evoke these repulsive spectral figures? Why does he conceive them? There must be something which makes him do so, though they have no real existence. He must feel the need of them, though they do not exist. Or perhaps is it just because of that? I do not understand it.

What can he be like, the being who produces

things like that, who revels in such horrors and lusts after them?

To look at, his arrogant face is admittedly both subtle and dignified, and it is unbelievable that he should have created these loathsome images. But it is so. It gives me much food for thought. He must have these gruesome creatures inside him like all the other things which he creates.

I must also recall his appearance when he was doing my portrait, how it changed until he became another person, with horrible sharp eyes, cold and unnatural, his whole face transformed into something cruel; he looked devilish.

He is not all that he makes himself out to be, as little, perhaps, as anybody else.

It is almost incredible that the same man should have done the Christ, sitting so pure and transfigured at His table of love.

ANGELICA went through the hall this evening and, as she passed by, the Prince told her to sit down for a moment with her embroidery. She was reluctant, though she dared not show it; she always avoids court life, nor is she suited to it nor fit to be exhibited as a princess. But who knows if she is the Prince's daughter? She may just as well be a bastard. But Messer Bernardo knows nothing of that. He looked at her as she sat there with downcast eyes and silly parted lips, looked and looked as though she were something extraordinary. But then to him everything is extraordinary: a freak of nature like myself, or one of his wonderful stones which are so rare that he picks them up from the ground to admire them. He kept silent and seemed quite moved, though she simply sat there without uttering a single word, giving every token of embarrassment. The sudden stop in the conversation was quite awkward.

I don't know what it was that affected him. Perhaps he pitied her for not being beautiful; he is a connoisseur of beauty and knows its importance. Perhaps that is why his gaze became so wistful and tender. I do not know, but neither do I care.

Naturally, the girl wanted to leave as soon as possible. She did not stay a minute longer than was absolutely necessary, but asked the Prince if she might go. On receiving his permission, she got up shyly and swiftly with her usual awkwardness, for her movements are still those of a child. It is strange that she should be so ungraceful.

As usual she was simply, almost commonly clad. She does not care about her dress, and neither does anybody else.

THE GREAT master Bernardo finds no peace of mind in his work. He goes from one thing to another, beginning, but never completing them.

Why? He ought to occupy himself exclusively with that Last Supper of his, so as to get it finished someday; but he does nothing of the kind. He must have wearied of it. Instead, he has begun a portrait of the Princess.

Apparently she does not want to be painted, but it is the Prince's wish. I understand her only too well! One may contemplate oneself in a mirror, but on leaving it one does not wish the reflection to remain there so that somebody else can take possession of it. I understand that, like me, she does not wish to be portrayed.

No one possesses himself! Detestable thought! No one possesses himself! Thus everything belongs to the others! Don't we own even our faces? Do they belong to anybody who chooses to look at them? And one's body? Can others own one's body? I find the notion most repellent.

I, and I alone, will be the sole possessor of that which is mine. Nobody else may seize it, none outrage it. It belongs to me and nobody else. And after my death I want to continue to own myself. Nobody is going to poke about in my entrails. I do not wish them to be seen by strangers, though they can scarcely be as revolting as those of that scoundrel Francesco.

Messer Bernardo's meddlings and his inquisitive interest in everything are repugnant to me. What is the use of it all? What sensible object does it serve? It repels me to think that he should have in his possession a portrait of me, that he should own me in this way. It is as though I were no longer sole owner of myself, as though I were also over there in Santa Croce, among his detestable monsters.

She can just as well be portrayed too! Why should she not endure the same insult as I? It gratifies me to think that she also will be exposed to his shameless scrutiny and take her turn in suffering his outrage.

But how can that strumpet be of any interest to him? I, who know her better than anybody else, have never found anything interesting about her.

We shall see what he will produce. After all, it has nothing to do with me. I don't think he is any judge of human nature.

MESSER BERNARDO has amazed me. He has amazed me so much that I have lain pondering it nearly all night.

They sat talking last night on their usual lofty topics. But one could see that he was plunged in gloom. He sat with his hand on his great beard, meditating and weighed down with thoughts which cannot have caused him much pleasure. But when he spoke he was filled with fire and passion, fire which was not visible from without, but seemed buried in ashes. He was unlike himself; one might have been listening to another man.

He said: "In the end human thought accomplishes so little. Its wings are strong, but not as strong as the destiny which gave them to us. It will not let us escape nor reach out any further than it desires. Our journey is predestined and, after a brief roaming which fills us with joy and expectation, we are drawn back again as the falcon is drawn back by the leash in the hand of the falconer. When shall we attain liberty? When will the leash be severed and the falcon soar into the open spaces?

"When? Will it ever be? Or is it not the secret of our being that we are and always will be bound to the hand of the falconer? If this were changed then we should cease to be human beings and our fate would not longer be that of humanity.

"And yet we are such that we are always subject to the enticement of space, and believe that we belong to it. And yet it is ever present over us, it reveals itself to us as something veritable. It is as real as our imprisonment."

He asked himself: "Why this limitless space to which we never can attain? What is the meaning of this unbounded immensity around us and around life, when we are such helpless prisoners and when life remains the same, no less enclosed within itself? What then is the use of the great dimensions?

Why should our little destiny, our narrow vale, be surrounded by such vastness? Does it add to our happiness? It does not appear so. It looks as though we were the unhappier for it."

I watched him closely, his somber mien and the strange weariness in his aged eyes.

He continued: "Are we the happier because we seek the truth? I know not. I merely seek it. All my life has been a restless search for it, and sometimes I have felt that I have apprehended it, I have caught a glimpse of its pure sky—but the sky has never opened itself for me, my eyes have never filled themselves with its endless spaces, without which nothing here can be fully understood. It is not vouchsafed to us. Therefore all my efforts really have been in vain. Therefore all that I have touched has been but partly true and partly completed. I think of my works with pain and so they will be regarded by all—as though it were a torso. All that I have created is imperfect and unfinished. All that I leave behind me is unfinished.

"But is there anything strange in that? It is the fate of mankind, the inescapable destiny of all human effort and all human achievement. Is it ever more than an attempt, an attempt at something which can never be achieved, which is not meant to be achieved by any of us? All human culture is but an attempt at something unattainable, something which far transcends our powers of realization. There it stands, mutilated, tragic as a torso. Is not the human spirit itself a torso?

"What use are wings when they can never be spread? They become a burden instead of a release. They weigh us down, we trail them and finally we hate them.

"And it comes as a relief when the falconer wearies of his cruel play and draws the hood over our head so that we no longer have to see anything."

He sat there dark and gloomy, with bitter lines about his mouth, and in his eyes a dangerous gleam. Upon my word, I was astounded. Was this the same man as he who not long ago stood entranced by the measureless greatness of man, who proclaimed the power of man, how man should reign like a mighty potentate in his vast kingdom, who depicted him almost as the peer of the gods?

I do not understand him. I understand nothing.

And the Prince sat there listening, fascinated by the words of his great master, though they were so unlike anything he had ever been known to say before. He seemed of the same opinion. One must confess that he certainly is teachable.

But how are these ideas connected? How can they combine such contradictions within themselves and talk about them all with the same profound conviction? I who am always the same, who am quite inalterable, find it utterly incomprehensible.

I have lain awake at night trying to understand them, but in vain. It is beyond me.

One minute it is a chorus of jubilation over the glory of being a human creature. The next minute it is nothing but hopelessness, complete futility, despair.

Well, what is it then?

H<small>E HAS</small> stopped working at the Princess' portrait. He says that he cannot complete it, that there is something about her which he cannot penetrate or explain to himself.

So it too will remain unfinished, like that Last Supper, like everything he begins.

I happened to see it once in the Prince's room, and I do not see what is wrong with it. I think it is admirable. He has painted her exactly as she is, like a middle-aged whore. It is really like her, diabolically so. The voluptuous face with the heavy eyelids and the vague lustful smile, everything is like her. And he has put all her soul into the picture; it is uncannily revealing.

After all he does seem to understand human nature.

What is lacking? He thinks that there is something lacking. But what? Something without which it is not really she, something essential? What can it be? I don't understand it at all.

But it must be unfinished since he says so. He has said that everything of his is left unfinished. Everything is but an attempt at something which can never be realized. All human culture is but an attempt, something quite impracticable. Therefore everything is really quite futile.

Of course it is. What would life be like if it were not futile? Futility is the foundation upon which it rests. On what other foundation could it have been based which would have held and never given way? A great idea can be undermined by another great idea and, in due course, be demolished by it. But futility is inaccessible, indestructible, immovable. It is a true foundation and that is why it has been chosen as such. That so much cogitation should be required to realize that!

I know that by instinct. It is my nature to know it.

SOMETHING is happening here, I know not what. I sense it like an unrest in the air—but what it is I do not know. Nothing is *actually* happening, but one feels as though something might.

On the surface everything is calm. Life in the palace goes on even more quietly than usual, because there are so few guests and no entertainments of any kind such as are customary at this time of year. But I don't know—this adds to the feeling that something special is brewing.

I am perpetually on my guard, observing everything—but there is nothing to observe. Nor can one see anything special out in the town. Everything is just as usual. But there is something! I am sure of it.

I must have patience and see what the future will bring.

Boccarossa, the condottiere, has left and the Palazzo Geraldi is empty again. Nobody knows where he has gone; it is as though the earth has swallowed him up. He may conceivably have had a dispute with the Prince. Many have found it strange that the latter with his great culture should consort so freely with such a coarse individual. I have not shared their opinion. Certainly Boccarossa is unusually crude and the Prince a notably polished cultivated man. But he too is of condottiere blood though most people seem to have forgotten it. It is not even so very long since they were condottieri, only a few generations. And what are a few generations?

I do not think that they have much difficulty in understanding each other.

Nothing happens, but the air is still tense. I can feel it, and in such matters I am never wrong. Something is going to happen here.

The Prince is almost feverishly busy. But with what? He receives a great many visitors and shuts himself up with them in secret council. Nothing transpires from these. What can they be about?

Courtiers arrive enveloped in secrecy; sometimes they are admitted into the palace at night. Many people come and go, whatever their business may be, governors, councilors, commanders, the chieftains of the ancient clans—the old warrior clans which once were subdued by the Prince's ancestors. The palace can no longer be called peaceful.

Maestro Bernardo does not seem to have anything to do with it. The Prince surrounds himself with persons of an entirely different type. The old scholar does not appear to be of any importance at all nowadays, at least not as important as he was before.

I cannot but approve of this. He has taken up too much room at this court.

My FEELING that something special was about to happen has proved to be correct. Without doubt such is the case.

Many details which cannot be ignored point to this. Astrologers have been summoned by the Prince and remained closeted with him, both the court astrologer Nicodemus and the other graybeards who batten on us here. This is an unmistakable sign. Too, the Prince has had several discussions with the Ambassador of the Medici and the representative of the Venetian shopkeepers' republic, even with the Archbishop who represents the Holy See. All this and a good deal more has been worthy of observation during the past few days and can have but one interpretation.

They must be planning a war. The astrologers have been summoned to discover whether the stars are favorable to such a scheme, for no wise prince will neglect such an elementary precaution. The poor wretches had been set aside in favor of Messer Bernardo, who also believes in the power of the stars but is said to hold different opinions on the subject, unorthodox notions which they regard as diabolical heresy. But now the Prince thinks it is safest to turn to the true believers. They go around bubbling over with their own importance. The negotiations with the envoys have taken place in order to assure the support or at least the good will of their respective states.

I should think that the attitude of the Holy Father toward these plans was the most important. No human project can succeed without the blessing of God.

I hope he has vouchsafed it; I long for the day when there will be war again!

IT IS going to be war! My nose, which is wise in such things, sniffs war everywhere, in the tension, the secrecy, the faces—in the very air we breathe which has something tantalizing about it that I recognize. Now we live again after this stifling time when nothing happened and which had to be eked out with endless prattle. It is good that at last people have something else to do.

In reality all of them want a war. It implies a simplification which comes as a relief. Everybody thinks that life is too complicated, and so it is as they live it. In itself life is not at all complicated; on the contrary its salient feature is its great simplicity, but they can never understand that. They do not realize that it is best when it is left as it is; they can never leave it in peace, or refrain from using it for a number of strange ends. But all the same they think that it is wonderful to be alive!

At last the Prince has roused himself from his stupor. His face is full of energy, with its short spade beard and lean pallid cheeks, the swift glance keeping almost imperceptible vigil like a bird of prey over its chosen territory. He must be about to hunt his favorite prey, the old archenemy of his clan.

Today I saw him hurrying up the palace steps closely followed by the Captain of the Guard. I think they had come from some military inspection. In the hall he threw his cloak to the servitors and stood there in his scarlet suit, strong and supple as a rapier, with a reckless smile on his thin lips. He looked as though he had just flung off a disguise, radiating unquenchable energy, in every way a man of action.

But I have always known that he was.

THE astrologers have declared that the times are particularly propitious to war, they could not have been better chosen. They have cast the Prince's horoscope and discovered that he was born under the sign of the Lion. That is nothing new; it has been common knowledge from his birth, when it is said to have greatly exercised the imagination of his entourage, being a good and promising omen for a prince and causing much wonder and some anxiety among the people. That is why he is called Leone. Mars is now in juxtaposition to the Lion and soon the war god's red star will reach the Prince's own powerful constellation. Other celestial phenomena which exercise an influence on the Prince's destiny are absolutely favorable, and so a happy issue to the campaign can be guaranteed. It would be almost unforgivable not to make use of such an unique opportunity.

Their predictions have not surprised me, for they always accord with the Prince's wishes, especially since his father once had a stargazer thrashed for maintaining that a misfortune threatened the dynasty. He had calculated that an evil star, trailing blood and fire behind it, had shown itself in the sky just as the founder of the family was making his bloodstained ascent to the throne. The prophecy has not come true, or not more than in any other princely dynasty.

No, I am not surprised and, for once, I am quite pleased with them. They are really skilled in their science and at last they have been of some use, for it is very important that the Prince, the soldiers and all the people should believe that the stars are favorable to their plans and interested in them. The stars now have spoken and everybody is very satisfied with what they have said.

I never converse with the stars, but these people do.

ONCE AGAIN Maestro Bernardo has astonished me. Last night the Prince and he had one of their long confidential discussions, and, as so often before, sat eagerly talking until late at night. This proves to me that the sage has not lost his significance nor has he, by his speculative broodings, segregated himself from the restless world of today. Not at all. I was thoroughly mistaken.

It annoys me when I make a mistake like that,

though nobody else can see through people and unmask them as I do.

When I was sent for, in order to wait on them as usual and fetch their wine goblets, they were both bending over some mysterious drawings which at first I could not understand. Later I got a better view of them and heard them being explained during the course of the conversation. They represented the most dreadful engines of war, intended to sow death and panic among the enemy; battle chariots to mow down the soldiery, furnished with long blades so that the ground about them was strewn with human limbs, and other devilish wheeled inventions to be propelled by galloping horses into the midst of the enemy's ranks. Nothing, not even the greatest courage, could stop these covered wagons filled with inaccessible marksmen which, according to his descriptions, would be able to break through the strongest array, after which the infantry could press forward and do their part. There were instruments of murder so appalling that I, alas, who have never been able to dedicate myself to the art of war, could not properly understand. Mortars, culverins, and falconets spewing fire and stones and cannon balls which severed the heads and arms of the soldiers were depicted realistically and clearly, as though their representation had been as absorbing as all the rest. He also gave a detailed description of the terrible destruction caused by these various engines, of the havoc they would wreak, and he told of all this as calmly and precisely as if he were dealing with any of the other matters in which he takes an interest. One realized that he wanted to see his machines in action, as was quite logical, since they are so wonderful and his own inventions.

Maestro Bernardo has been planning this simultaneously with his other occupations, his nature studies when he examined his extraordinary pebbles and pulled his flowers apart, and his ferreting in Francesco's body, which I remember him describing to the Prince as one of nature's great unfathomable masterpieces and his picture of the Last Supper in Santa Croce with the celestial Christ sitting among His disciples at their love feast with Judas the betrayer crouched in his far corner.

He has been equally attracted and preoccupied by all these things, so why should he not be just as entranced by his marvelous machines? It may be that the human body is a most ingenious construction, though I cannot look upon it as such. But so is such an instrument and, again, it is his very own discovery.

Oddly enough the Prince was not so interested in those terrible contrivances which to my mind would be the most effective and which by their appearance alone might stampede a whole army;

he preferred the less impressive ones which did not testify to such a macabre and powerful imagination, but which he maintained would be even more efficacious. He observed that the ghastliest of all were more suited to the future, but anything which could possibly be put into practice would be used. Grapnels for the investment of a fortress, a remarkable method of mining bastions and blowing them up, ingenious improvements for catapults and ordnance unknown to the enemy —clearly all these matters already had been fully discussed and partially exploited by them.

All this impressive material—the incredible profusion of ideas and inventions, the fertile, seemingly boundless inspiration—aroused the Prince's deepest admiration, and he was enthusiastic in his praises of the master's genius. Never before had he given such proof of the range of his imagination and ingenuity! All that evening they plunged into the tantalizing realm of fantasy, exchanging opinions as eagerly as during one of the most profitable evenings they had spent before. And I listened to them with pleasure, for I too for once was filled with delight and admiration.

Now I know why the Prince summoned the great Messer Bernardo, and why he has always treated him as an equal during his stay and always shown him such deep appreciation and flattering attention. I understand his burning interest in all

Bernardo's scholarly efforts, for his nature studies, his incredible knowledge which includes the practical and the useless, and that sensitive admiring verdict on the master's art, his Last Supper in Santa Croce, and all the other works of the learned man. I undertsand it all!

He is a great prince!

LAST NIGHT I had a horrible dream. I thought that I saw Maestro Bernardo standing on a high mountain, tall and imposing with his gray hair and his mighty brow, but the air about his head was full of monsters flapping on bats' wings, all the foul freaks which I knew from his drawings in Santa Croce. They fluttered about him like imps and it seemed as though he were their master. Their ghostly faces resembled those of lizards and toads, but his remained grave, stern and noble. He seemed just the same as usual. Then, by slow degrees, his body underwent a change. It became shrunken and misshapen, and crumpled wings sprouted forth which joined to the thin hairy legs like those of a bat. His face was as solemn as before, but he began to flutter his wings and suddenly he rose and flew away with the other gruesome creatures into the darkness of the night.

I do not bother about dreams; they mean nothing

and make no difference. Reality is the only thing that matters.

Obviously he must be misshapen; I decided that long ago.

Boccarossa has crossed the frontier at the head of four thousand men! Already he is four leagues from the border and il Toro has not yet recovered from the surprise attack!

Such is the tremendous news which aroused the town today like a thunderclap, the unprecedented occurrence which preoccupies all minds!

The great condottiere had assembled his mercenaries in deepest secrecy in the inaccessible mountain districts at the southwest frontier, and prepared the successful invasion with diabolical cunning. Nobody suspected a thing, not even we ourselves. Only the Prince, the originator of the masterly plan of attack! It is almost inconceivable! One scarcely dares believe it!

Now the days of the Montanzas draw to a close, and the detestable Lodovico, who is reported to be as hated by his own people as by us, will at last crack his bull neck and shut up the story of his shameless clan.

He has been completely hoodwinked, the cunning scoundrel! Undoubtedly he suspected that the Prince was planning to attack him, but he knew that no army was being set up here, and so he was lulled into security. And least of all did he expect an onslaught in that part of the country where the ground is so impassable and where he has no border fortresses! It is the end of il Toro! His day of reckoning has come!

The atmosphere in the town is indescribable. People crowd excitedly together in the streets, gesticulating and talking; or they stand in silence watching the troops march by, the Prince's own troops which are now being concentrated, though no one knows where they have come from. It is as though they had sprung from the earth. One can see that everything was very carefully and secretly prepared. All the bells are ringing and the churches are crammed to bursting. The priests pray earnestly for the war and obviously it has the blessing of the church. How could it be otherwise? This is going to be a glorious war!

All the people are rejoicing, and here at court there is no limit to the admiration and enthusiasm for the Prince.

O<small>UR OWN</small> troops are going to another sector. They will cross the border to the east in the broad river valley, the old classic road of attack. It is only a day's march away, and there on the level, where the ground is suited to a regular battle and the soil watered with glorious blood, they will join up with the condottiere's army. That is the plan of campaign! I have worked it out!

I do not *know* for certain that that is the plan, but I have picked up bits here and there and come to that conclusion. I am busy finding out everything, keeping up with everything, listening at keyholes, hiding behind cupboards and curtains to hear as much as possible of the great impending events.

What a plan of attack! And of course it must succeed. There are fortresses on that section of the border, but they will fall. Maybe they will surrender straightway, knowing the hopelessness of resistance. Maybe they will be stormed. In any case, they will not stop us. Nothing can stop us, since the initial assault came as such a surprise, catching them unawares.

And the Prince—what a general! What a sly fox! Such cunning, such foresight! And what grandeur in the whole plan of campaign!

It fills me with pride to be the dwarf of such a prince.

I can think of one thing only: how can I go to the war? I *must*. But how? How can my dream be realized? I have no military training in the ordinary sense such as is necessary to an officer or even a common soldier. But I can bear arms! And fence like a man! My rapier is as good as anybody's! Maybe not quite so long, but a short sword is not the least dangerous! The enemy will soon find that out!

This constant brooding makes me ill, the fear of being left behind with the women and children, of not being allowed to go along when at last something is actually happening. And the bloodiest slaughter may be just now, at the very beginning.

I crave blood!

I AM GOING with them! I *am* going with them!

This morning I plucked up my courage and confided in the Prince, telling him my burning wish to share in the campaign. I presented my request with such passion that it made an obvious impression on him. Also I was fortunate enough to arrive at a time when he was in a particularly favorable mood. He passed his hand over his cropped fringed hair as is his wont when in good humor and his black eyes glittered as he looked at me.

Naturally I could go to war, he said. He was going himself and would take me along as a matter of course. Can a prince be without his dwarf? Who else would pour his wine, he added, smiling at me.

I am going with them! I am going with them!

At PRESENT I am in a tent on a mound with a few pine trees, from which one has an excellent view of the enemy on the level ground below. The tent is in the Prince's colors, striped with red and yellow, and its rattlings are as stimulating as a fanfare of trumpets. I am fully armed, just like the Prince, with breastplate and helmet, and my sword in a silver baldric by my side. It is near sunset, and for the moment I am alone. I can hear the officers' voices planning the morrow's attack, and in the distance the gay melodious songs of the soldiers. I can glimpse il Toro's black-and-white tent down below and the men about it looking so small as to be innocuous; far off to the left are unarmed knights, stripped to the waist, watering their horses in the river.

We have been in the field for more than a week, and the time has been crammed with great happenings. The campaign has developed exactly as I prophesied. We stormed the border forts after bombarding them with Messer Bernardo's excellent culverins; the effect of their awe-inspiring cannonade was unsurpassed, and terrorized the garrison into surrender. Il Toro sent inadequate troops against us, taken from the forces with which he was trying to check Boccarossa's advance, and we have fought some fierce skirmishes with them. However, they were vastly inferior to us, so the victory has always been ours. During this time Boccarossa's army, opposed to ever weakening and dwindling troops, has pressed forward over the lowlands, burning and pillaging and always bearing north in order to make contact with us. This longed-for and vital objective was attained at midday yesterday, and now we stand together on the slopes between the lowland and the mountains, a combined host of more than fifteen thousand men, including two thousand horsemen.

I was present at the meeting between the Prince and his condottiere. It was a historic moment, never to be forgotten. The Prince, who has been rejuvenated these days in a manner which arouses general admiration, was clad in a suit of splendid armor, with breastplate and armpieces of silver gilt. On his helmet were plumes of yellow and red which dipped and swayed as, surrounded by his foremost captains, he courteously greeted his celebrated brother in arms. For once there was a faint color on his pale and aristocratic face and the thin lips were curved in a candid and friendly smile which, like everything else connected with him, was yet reticent and somewhat cautious. Opposite him stood Boccarossa, broad and powerful, with a body that, to me, seemed gigantic. I had a peculiar sensation of never having seen him before. He had come straight from the battle. He wore steel armor, very plain in comparison with that of the Prince, and its only adornment was a beast's head in bronze on the cuirass, an enraged lion whose tongue protruded from its gaping jaws. His helmet had no crest and no ornament of any kind, but fitted close to that head of his which seemed the most terrifying I had ever seen. The jaw alone of that fat pockmarked visage was enough to inspire awe; the thick blackish red lips were pressed together into a mouth which seemed incapable of opening, and the expression which crouched brooding within the eyes might force an adversary into submission without ever leaving them, merely by showing that it was there. He was a frightening sight, but more of a *man* than anybody else whom I ever have met. I must admit that he made such an impression on me that I may never be able to rid myself of it. He was a revelation of something—I know not what. Perhaps of humanity when it really is capable of something. As though bewitched, I stood and scrutinized him with that ancient gaze of mine which has already witnessed everything, with my dwarf's eyes in which all the centuries dwell.

He was taciturn, said practically nothing. It was the others who spoke. Once he smiled at some utterance of the Prince. I do not know why I say that he smiled—but it was an expression that, on another face, might have been called a smile.

I wonder if, like me, he cannot smile?

He is no smooth-face like the rest and no newborn babe either, but of ancient race, though not so old as my own.

The Prince seemed somewhat insignificant beside him, and I admit it, despite my great admiration for my lord, which I have often emphasized, particularly of late.

I hope that I may see him in combat.

For the great battle is to take place tomorrow morning. One might think that the attack should have been made at once, as soon as the two armies had met, and before Lodovico had had a chance to take breath and assemble his scattered forces, as now he has been able to. I pointed this out to the Prince, but he replied that the men must have a rest first. Besides, one must be chivalrous to one's opponent and give him time to get into battle array before starting such a momentous action. I expressed my doubts as to the wisdom and justification of such a strategy. He answered: "Wise or not, I am a knight and must act as such. You do not have to." I shook my head. There is no understanding the character of that peculiar man. I wonder what Boccarossa thinks of it all.

There can be no doubt that il Toro has put his respite to good account. All day we have been able to see it from up here. He even has been able to procure reinforcements.

But we shall win; that goes without saying. And it may be an advantage if he collects as many men as possible, since that makes all the more for us to slay. The greater the enemy, the greater the victory. He ought to realize that he will be defeated anyhow and that, therefore, it would be better not to have so many men. But he is overconfident and as obstinate as a mule.

But it would be wrong to think that he is not dangerous. He is sly, cunning, and ruthless, a really fine general. He would be a terrible adversary if the war had not caught him unawares. The significance of our surprise attack becomes more and more evident and doubtless we shall be reminded of it during the whole campaign.

I know all the details of the plan for tomorrow's attack. Our—that is to say, the Prince's—army, will attack their center, Boccarossa's, their left wing. We shall form not one but two fronts, as is quite natural, since we have two armies at our disposition. The enemy who has but one will be compelled to fight on two fronts, and obviously he will thereby encounter many difficulties which we shall avoid. There can be no doubt of the outcome, but we must be prepared for certain losses. I think it will be a bloody business, but nothing can be achieved without sacrifice. And this battle is so vitally important that its outcome will probably decide the future course of the war. In such circumstances it is worth while to sacrifice a good deal.

The secrets of warfare, once a sealed book to me, interest me more and more. And the ups and downs of life in the field appeal to me enormously. It is a marvelous life! Body and soul feel liberated when you take part in war. One becomes a new man. I have never felt so well. I breathe so easily, I move so easily. It is as though my body were as light as air.

Never in all my life have I been so happy. I even feel as though I had never been happy before.

Tomorrow! Tomorrow!

I am as happy as a child at the thought of the battle.

I jot down a few lines in haste.

We have won a victory, a glorious victory! The enemy is retreating in disarray and trying in vain to reassemble his scattered troops. We are following them up! The road to Montanza's hitherto unconquered city lies open before us.

As soon as events permit I shall give a detailed description of the wonderful engagement.

Events speak for themselves, words have no further meaning. I have exchanged the pen for the sword.

At last I have leisure to write. We have been fighting and advancing all the time for several days and it has been impossible to give a thought to anything else. Sometimes we have not even had time to pitch a tent for the night, but have camped in the open among the vineyards and the olive groves, wrapped in our cloaks, pillowing our heads on stones. A wonderful life! But now it is a little calmer. The Prince says we need a breathing space and he may be right. Even perpetual successes can be exhausting in the long run.

Now we are only a league from the town and can see it lying before us with its towers and battlements, its churches and belfries and Montanza's old castle on a rise in the center with other smaller houses clustering around, the whole surrounded by a high wall. A veritable nest of robbers! We can hear the pealing of the church bells, presumably calling upon God to save them. We shall see to it that he has no opportunity of granting their prayers. Il Toro has assembled the remnants of his army here, between us and the city. He has rounded up all the men he can get hold of, but they will not suffice for he has already been too badly mauled. Once more the outcome is a certainty. A great commander like that ought to realize the hopelessness of his position. Apparently he intends to do his best and mobilize his uttermost resources in the hope of cheating fate. This is his last attempt to save the city.

Rather a hopeless attempt. The fate of the Montanzas was decided on a historic morning nearly a week ago. Now only the final settlement remains.

I shall try to give a detailed and authentic description of the great incomparable battle.

It began with a joint attack from both our armies, exactly as I had predicted. Seen from the slopes, it was a magnificent spectacle, a feast for all the senses. Martial music resounded, the standard was unfurled, the banners waved over the orderly and colorful ranks. The silver bugle echoed over the countryside in the dawning, and the infantry poured down the slopes. The enemy awaited them ranged in close and somewhat threatening formations, and the strongly armed adversaries closed in on each other. From the start it was a bloody business. There were casualties on both sides, the wounded were stabbed or trampled to death as they tried to crawl away, and the usual cries and moans were heard. The fighting shifted to and fro; sometimes our men seemed to have the upper hand, elsewhere the enemy was superior. To begin with, Boccarossa pretended to take the same line as we, but by degrees his troops swung in a wide arc and fell upon the enemy's wing. This dangerous maneuver caught them unawares, and they had great difficulty in defending themselves. Victory was within reach, or so it appeared to me. By now several hours had passed and the sun was high in the heavens.

Suddenly something terrible happened. Those

of our troops who were nearest the river began to weaken. They yielded to the pressure of il Toro's right wing and allowed themselves to be driven backward, making only the clumsiest and feeblest attempts to stand. They seemed to have lost all their fighting spirit, merely went on retreating, ready to face anything rather than death. I could not believe my eyes. I could not grasp what was going on down there, particularly as we were numerically superior, actually about twice as many as the others. I felt my blood boil with shame over their incredible cowardice. I raved and shrieked and stamped, shaking my fists in helpless fury, showering abuse on them, screaming my anger and contempt. But what was the use? Of course they did not hear me and merely continued to withdraw. I thought I should go out of my mind. And nobody came to reinforce them! Nobody seemed to pay the slightest attention to their predicament. Not that they deserved it!

Suddenly I saw the Prince, who was commanding the center, signal to some detachments to the rear of the center. They started to move forward at an angle toward the river, and with renewed vigor began to break through the enemy's lines. Step by step, with irresistible strength, they fought their way until, with a wild bellow of joy, they reached the river bank. They had cut off the retreat of between five and seven hundred men who were thereby completely hedged in with no prospect but immediate annihilation.

I was overcome with amazement. I had had no suspicion of this ruse! I had taken it for cowardice. My heart thumped, my breast swelled with joy. I felt a wonderful sense of relief after the terrible strain.

A dramatic scene followed. Our troops pressed in from every side, forcing the surrounded foe together and backward between the front line and the river bank. At last they were packed so closely together that they could scarcely move, and we began to destroy them. It was a massacre the like of which I have never seen, and not only a massacre, for they were driven out into the river where they drowned like rats. They fought for dear life in the current, flailing the water with their arms, yelling for help and altogether behaving in a most unsoldierly fashion. Hardly any of them could swim; it was as though they had never seen water before. Those who could crawl ashore were promptly cut down, and those who tried to reach the other bank were carried away by the fierce current. Scarcely any escaped alive.

Our disgrace was transformed into a splendid victory!

Developments followed each other at a tremendous pace. Our center stormed down on the enemy, followed by the left wing, while, on the right,

Boccarossa's troops slashed away with renewed and frenzied energy. And from the hills fresh cavalry squadrons came charging down with their lances in rest, and joined in the melee, completely demoralizing il Toro's exhausted wavering army. Soon their desperate defense was turned into disorderly flight, and we pursued them with the horsemen in the van, to squeeze the last drops from our matchless victory. The Prince was determined to profit by every opportunity. Part of his force, including infantry and cavalry, was sent in a different direction from the others, and went off down one of the side valleys with the obvious purpose of overtaking the enemy. The mountains concealed their further movements so we could not see exactly what happened next. They disappeared among the vine-clad hills on the other side of the level ground which had been the scene of the battle.

Now we began to stir ourselves in the camp. Horses were harnessed to the wagons, and everything was hastily packed onto them, stores and armaments of every description; everybody rushed wildly about, the baggage was to be sent away. I sat at the back of the cart on which the Prince's tent had been placed. The signal was given and we drove down the slope and on to the battlefield. It was deserted, save for the dead and wounded who lay so close together that we could hardly proceed without sometimes driving over them. Most of them were already dead, but the others moaned and sighed without ceasing. Our own men called to us to take them along, but it was impossible, for we must hasten to catch up with the army. In war one becomes hardened, inured to everything, but I had never known anything like this before. I saw some horses among the corpses. We drove past one that had had its belly split open so that the entrails lay on the ground. The sight made me feel sick and I feared I might vomit. I do not know what came over me; I called to the driver to increase his pace; he cracked his whip and we rolled on.

It is very strange. I have often noticed that in some respects I am peculiarly sensitive. I find certain things quite unendurable. It is the same whenever I think of Francesco's intestines. Some things, though perhaps quite natural in themselves, are really extraordinarily nauseating.

The day was drawing to a close. Even a day like this must have an end. The sun was low above the western hills and its dying rays fell over the field which had witnessed so much glory, heroism, and defeat. Twilight began to cover it as I sat there in the jolting wagon, looking backward.

The scene was enveloped in darkness and the bloody drama which had been enacted there was already a part of history.

I HAVE had plenty of time for writing, because it rains without stopping, pouring down for days on end as though the heavens had been opened. We are deluged unceasingly.

This, of course, is tiresome. Everything in camp is dirty and muddy. The tent lanes are knee-deep in clay, and equine and human excrement floats about in the mire. Everything one touches is wet and filthy and feels disgusting and if one goes out for a moment one is immediately soaked to the skin. The tent roofs leak and inside it is like a morass. All this is very unpleasant and not at all good for morale. Every evening we hope that tomorrow will be fine, but as soon as we wake up we hear the same pattering on the canvas.

I do not see the point of this eternal rain. It impedes all warfare and puts a stop to the whole campaign. And just when we were going to garner the fruits of our great successes. *Why* is it raining?

The soldiers are out of sorts. They spend their days sleeping or throwing dice. Naturally there can be no martial spirit under such conditions. We can be sure that all this time il Toro is reinforcing his troops, whereas we are not getting any stronger. Not that it worries me, but the thought of it is irritating just the same.

Nothing has such an injurious effect on an army's morale as rain. The excitement of the game fades away and the glamour disappears, all the glitter and stimulus which are part of warfare. The power and the glory have departed. But there should be a reaction against this picture of war as an uninterrupted carnival. War is not a pastime, it is deadly serious. It is death, defeat, destruction. It is no agreeable life, no jousting with an opponent who is perhaps perpetually inferior. One must school oneself to endure everything, toil, hardship, suffering of every kind. That is absolutely necessary.

It can be dangerous if this depression spreads itself among the troops. Much still lies ahead before we can achieve the final victory. The enemy is not quite routed, although he soon will be. And we must admit that he made rather a skillful retreat after the terrible defeat at the river, and prevented us from actually capturing him. And now, as I have pointed out, he is sure to be mustering new forces. We shall need all our old fighting spirit to put an end to him.

But the Prince is not in the least dispirited. He is one of those who really love war in all its forms. He is calm, self-confident, and energetic, and his temperament is unchanging in its serenity. He is always filled with courage and absolutely sure of victory. A marvelous warrior! In the field he and I really resemble one another.

I have only one grudge against him which I cannot overlook and for which I constantly reproach him; that is his refusal to let me join in the fighting. I cannot understand why he refuses my request, why he prevents me! Before every battle I have begged and implored him, once I even besought him on my knees, clasping his legs and bathing them with my tears. But he always pretends not to hear me or merely smiles and says something about my being too precious, that something might happen to me. Happen! I ask nothing better! He does not realize what this means to me, that I crave combat with all my soul, more so than any of his soldiers, with a deeper and more burning passion than they. War is no game to me, but grim reality. I want to fight, I want to *kill!* Not for the glory of it, but for the *deed* alone! I want to see men fall, see death and destruction around me. He knows nothing about me! And so he lets me pour his wine and wait upon him, and forbids me to leave the tent and join in the fray where I so long to be. I must stand about and look on while others perform the deeds which are never out of my thoughts, but I may never share in the battle. It is so unbearably humiliating! Why, I have not yet killed a man, not a single one! He has no notion of the suffering which he causes me.

So I am not absolutely truthful when I call myself really happy.

Others besides the Prince have noticed my martial spirit, but they do not know as he does how serious it is, how deeply rooted in my being. They only see me going about in sword and armor and it catches their attention. Their opinion of me and my share in the campaign is of no significance whatsoever.

Naturally, I know many of the people here, courtiers and others who were always at the palace, renowned scions of ancient families famous in warfare throughout the centuries, noble lords exercising high commands thanks to their social position. I am well acquainted with all the superior officers and, of course, they know me too. They and the Prince are the real leaders and one must admit that he has surrounded himself with a magnificent collection of the old fighting nobility.

Don Riccardo's share in the campaign irritates me. He is everywhere, boasting and swaggering, preferably in the vicinity of the Prince, full of silly jests which arouse the coarse laughter of his associates. He looks extraordinarily foolish with his fresh peasant complexion which is far too ruddy, and his big white teeth which are constantly in evidence, for he laughs at everything. His way of tossing his head and twisting the curls of his black beard is quite unbearable. I cannot understand how the Prince can stand having him in the neighborhood.

Still less can I understand how the Princess can

see any charm in this vulgarian, for vulgar he is despite his pedigree. Still, that has nothing to do with me nor with anything else, for that matter, and in point of fact is of no interest to me.

When they call him brave I, at least, do not understand what they are talking about. He was in the fighting at the river like all the others, but I do not believe that he distinguished himself in any way. I never caught a glimpse of him. Presumably he has told everybody how brave he was, and as they all listen whenever he opens his mouth, he has gained their credence. Personally, I do not for one moment believe in his courage. He is an intolerable braggart—that's what he is!

He a hero! The mere idea is ridiculous!

Ah, but the Prince is brave. He is always in the melee. One can see his white charger and distinctive crest in the thick of the battle, and the enemy can see them too. He is always exposing himself to mortal danger. One can see that he loves a hand-to-hand fight for its own sake; he rejoices in it. And, of course, Boccarossa is brave, if bravery be the right word. It seems too inadequate and fails to give a true picture of him in action. They tell me that his tactics are enough to terrify the most hardened warrior and, most terrifying of all, he does not seem in the least maddened or agitated by the fighting, but bites his lips together and calmly pursues his trade of cold-blooded and methodical slaughter. Often he fights afoot so as to be nearer his victim. He seems to enjoy the carnage and revels in cutting down his man. In comparison, the methods of the Prince and the others seem like child's play. I speak from hearsay, for I have always been too far away to see it for myself. I cannot describe my vexation when I think of what I have missed.

Men like the Prince and Boccarossa are brave, each in his own way, but Don Riccardo! It is grotesque to mention his name in the same breath.

Boccarossa and his men enjoy harrying the land through which they pass, burning and plundering rather more than the Prince considers necessary. He too, of course, realizes that plunder is part of warfare. Where they have passed they leave practically nothing living behind them, and it is said that the Prince and his condottiere are not of the same mind on this point. I must say that I incline to Boccarossa's theory. Enemy country is enemy country and must be treated as such. That is the law of war. It may seem cruel, but war and cruelty go together; there is no getting away from it. One must exterminate the people against whom one is fighting and ravage the land so that it cannot rise again. It can be very dangerous to leave a few opposition centers in the rear; one must know that one's back is free. I am sure that Boccarossa is right.

[89]

Sometimes the Prince seems to forget that he is in the midst of the enemy. Now and then he treats the population in a manner of which one cannot possibly approve. For example, when he came to the dirty mountain village, he stayed to watch their rustic feast and listen to their flute players as though he thought their music worth hearing. I could not understand how he could take any pleasure in it and how he could bring himself to speak to these dolts. That sort of thing passes my understanding, nor did I understand what they were doing, though according to their own account it was some kind of feast to celebrate the harvest. A pregnant woman poured wine and olive oil over the earth on a bit of tilled ground, and then they all seated themselves in a circle around it and partook of bread and wine and goats' milk cheese.

The Prince sat down too and ate with them, praising their olives and the cheese which looked dry and nasty. When the dirty old earthen pitcher of wine reached him he set it to his lips and drank like the others. It was a distasteful sight. Never had I seen him behave like that, nor believed that he could do so. He never ceases to surprise me in one way or another.

When he asked them why the woman had done all that, they became very secretive and embarrassed and did not want to answer, but smiled knowingly with their silly peasant faces. But at last they came out with it: it was to make the earth bear grapes and olives the next year also. It sounded too comic for words. As though the earth could know that they had poured wine and oil on it and their purpose in so doing! "We do this every year at this time," they said. And an old man with a long tangled beard, splashed with wine, approached the Prince, bent his head and gazed candidly into his eyes. "So have our fathers done," he said, "and we do the same."

Then they got up and began to dance, clumsily and loutishly, old and young, even the poor old man who was already on the brink of the grave. And the flute players played on their homemade pipes which had a few notes only which were repeated again and again. I could not understand how the Prince could wish to listen to this artless music, but both he and Don Riccardo, who was present too (when is he not?), lingered there forgetting that a war was going on and that they were in the midst of the enemy. And when the people began to sing their gloomy monotonous songs they could not tear themselves away, but remained until twilight fell and they were compelled to leave. Then perhaps they realized that it might be dangerous to stay up there in the encroaching darkness.

"What a beautiful evening," they said to each other, when at last we went back to camp. And

Don Riccardo, who must give proof of his sensibility in and out of season, began to expatiate most fulsomely on the beauty of the scenery, though there was nothing particularly pretty about it, and stopped time and again to listen to the flutes and songs from the village with its dirty old houses perched up on the mountainside.

That same evening he brought two harlots into the Prince's tent; he had found them in the camp whither they had contrived to worm their way from the town, presumably because they hoped to receive better pay here where there was a shortage of their kind. "Also it is more fitting for a woman to lie with an enemy," they said. At first the Prince seemed shocked and I was sure he would be angry and chase them away and punish Don Riccardo severely for his incredible impudence, but to my intense astonishment he suddenly burst out laughing, took one of them on his knee and called for our rarest wine. I have not yet recovered from my amazement over the things which I was forced to witness that night. I would give much never to have been there and to be quit of these revolting memories. If I could discover how they came here! But women, especially women of their kind, are like rats; they admit of no obstacles but gnaw their way through everything. I was about to leave and go to bed in the servitors' tent, but now I felt compelled to remain and serve not only my lord and

Don Riccardo, but also these painted strumpets who stank of Venetian pomades and hot fat female flesh. I found it extraordinarily repulsive.

Don Riccardo descanted on their beauty and had no words fair enough for one—for her eyes and hair and her legs which he showed to the Prince though she tried to stop him; but then he turned to the other and praised her in equally flattering terms so that she should not feel left in the cold. "All women are beautiful!" he cried. "They are the source of all the sweetness of life! But sweetest of all is the courtesan whose life is dedicated to love and who never plays it false." His behavior was so idiotic and tasteless that even I, who have always regarded him as the stupidest of vulgarians, would never have believed him capable of such grotesque buffoonery.

They drank a great deal of wine and gradually it took effect. Don Riccardo became sickly sentimental and began to babble of love and recite reams of appalling poetry, mostly love sonnets, to somebody whom he called Laura, so that the women's eyes filled with tears. He and the Prince lay with their heads on the laps of these trollops who tenderly stroked their hair and sighed sweetly as they listened to Don Riccardo's flummery. He had chosen the prettier of the two, and I could not avoid seeing the peculiar way in which the Prince looked at him both then and later on during the evening, when the stupid women seemed most bewitched by him and his antics. Women always prefer the silliest and most insignificant men, because they remind them of themselves.

But suddenly he sprang up and declared that now they had had enough of lachrymose lyrics, now they were going to drink and be merry! This marked the beginning of an orgy of wine-bibbing and jesting and laughter and indecent gestures and foul stories of a coarseness that I cannot reproduce. When the carousal was at its height the Prince raised his glass and toasted Don Riccardo: "Tomorrow you shall be my standard-bearer in the battle!" The other was delighted at this unexpected honor and his eyes glittered. "I hope it will be dangerous!" he exclaimed, preening himself before the women so that they should see how brave he was. "One never knows, it may well be," replied the Prince. Don Riccardo seized his hand and kissed it in humble gratitude like a squire before his liege lord. "Beloved Prince, remember what you have promised me in the midst of the festal gaiety." "Rest assured that I shall not forget it."

The courtesans found all this very impressive and looked on with eager eyes, but their first glance was for him who should bear the standard in the battle.

After this interlude they went on with their disgusting orgy and their behavior became more and more offensive and shameless, so that I who was forced to witness it was filled with confusion and nausea. They kissed and hugged each other, with flushed faces, hot and panting with lust. It was indescribably nasty. Despite the women's pretended resistance, they pulled down their dresses, exposing their naked breasts. The prettier had rose pink nipples with a mole beside one of them, not very big, but it was impossible to avoid noticing it. When I came forward to serve her I was nauseated by the smell of her body which was just the same as that of the Princess when she lies in bed in the morning, though I have never been so close to her. When Don Riccardo took hold of her breasts I felt such a distaste and hatred for the lecher that I would fain have throttled him with my bare hands or killed him with my dagger so as to drain the prurient blood from his body and stop him from ever embracing a woman again. I stood there filled with sick loathing and pondered over the offensiveness of mankind. May all these beings end up in the fires of hell!

At last Don Riccardo had one of his idiotic ideas. He had been most with the prettier, for she would not leave him in peace, but now he proposed that he and the Prince throw dice to see which one should have her. Everybody approved of this, including the Prince, and the woman shrieked with laughter and wriggled her naked torso in her delight at being the object of such a duel. I found her disgusting and I could not understand how they could consider her beautiful and desirable, or how they could compete for such a repulsive prize. She was blonde and fair-skinned with great blue eyes and quantities of hair in her armpits. I found her loathsome. I have never known why it is people have hair under their arms, and I feel squeamish when I see it, particularly if it is moist. We dwarfs have nothing like that and we find it nasty and offensive. If I had hair there or on any part of my body except my head, where hair is meant to grow, I should feel intensely ashamed.

I had to fetch the dice, and the Prince threw first and turned up a six and a one. She was to go to the one who first reached fifty. They went on turn and about, and the women hung over them, deeply interested in the result and commenting on the fluctuations of the game with shameless remarks, squeals and guffaws. The Prince won, and they all arose, screeching and laughing at each other.

Immediately afterward they flung themselves upon the women, each on his chosen one, dragged off their clothes and began to behave in such an incredibly abhorrent fashion that I could bear it no longer, but rushed out of the tent and had scarcely passed its door before I vomited the soul out of my body. I was cold all over and my skin felt granulated like that of a plucked chicken. Shaking violently, I huddled down in the hay between the cook and the horrible groom who stinks of horses and always kicks me in the morning when he gets up. I don't know why; he says that he likes kicking me just then.

I cannot understand the love that human beings feel for each other. It merely revolts me. All that I have witnessed this evening has revolted me.

It may be because I am another kind of being, subtler, more sensitive, and therefore I react against many things which do not appear to affect them. I do not know. I have no experience of what they call love, nor do I wish to try it. Once they offered me a female dwarf, a lovely woman with small penetrating eyes like mine and a withered face and body like ancient parchment, exactly as a human being should be. But she aroused no passion in me, though I could see that there was nothing repellent about her beauty, that it was not like theirs. It may have been because it was the Princess who offered her, wanting to bring us together like any old procuress, for she hoped that we would produce a dwarf child for her, and at that moment she had set her heart on having one. It was before Angelica was born and she wanted something to play with. She said that she thought a dwarf child would be so amusing. But I had no wish to pander to her whims, nor would I degrade our tribe by falling in with her shameful proposal.

Incidentally, she was wrong when she thought we would give her a child. We dwarfs beget no young, we are sterile by virtue of our own nature. We have nothing to do with the perpetuation of life; we do not even desire it. We have no need to be fertile, for the human race itself produces its own dwarfs, of that one may be sure. We let ourselves be born of these haughty creatures, with the same pangs as they. Our race is perpetuated through them, and thus and thus only can we enter this world. That is the inner reason for our sterility. We belong to that race and at the same time we stand outside it. We are guests on a visit. Ancient wizened guests on a visit which has lasted for thousands of years.

But my reflections have carried me away from the subject of my present narrative. I did not mean to write about all that.

Sure enough, next morning Don Riccardo bore the princely standard. There has been a great deal of talk about the events connected with this and certain circumstances in the battle, but, of course, I have my own opinion about all this and what there may be behind it. They say that by an unaccountable order the Prince unnecessarily jeopardized Don Riccardo's life, that at one time it was taken for granted that he must be killed when, with his comparatively small troop of horses, he was forced into an extremely perilous situation. And they say that he fought with the utmost gallantry, though I do not believe a word of that. He is said to have assembled his few remaining men around the standard and defended it against the superior enemy forces. But when the fighting took such a dangerous turn the Prince rushed there, either because he could not resist the lure of such hazardous play, or for some other reason. Followed by a handful of men he plunged into the midst of the enemy surrounding Don Riccardo as though to succor him, when suddenly his horse received a pike in the ribs and fell to the ground. The Prince was thrown and lay there in the thick of the melee. This inspired Don Riccardo to such frenzy and "courage" that he and his men broke their way out of the ring and, with the strength of despair and the aid of the Prince's horsemen, contrived to hold the adversary in check until they were relieved by fresh troops. By then Don Riccardo was covered with wounds. It is insinuated that he must have realized that the Prince wanted him to be killed, but nevertheless he acted as he did and saved his master's life.

That is the report which I do not believe. In many respects, it seems most unlikely, and I merely relate it, because it is the version of this morning's dramatic events which is current here. I have a very different opinion which is principally grounded on my detailed personal knowledge of Don Riccardo. I know him better than anyone else; he is not like that.

The report is obviously colored by the general notion of Don Riccardo and his own conceit of himself. It has become a kind of legend, which nobody troubles to investigate, that he is the embodiment of courage and that all his acts are noble and magnificent. The sole ground for all this is his inimitable talent for showing off and attracting all attention to himself. His absurd vanity is as apparent in his soldiering as in his general behavior, and the recklessness which they all admire is part of his stupidity. They confuse foolhardiness with courage.

If he really is as brave as he says and really is always exposing himself to every conceivable danger, why doesn't he get killed? One may well ask. Nobody would miss him, at least not I.

Now he is said to be wounded in many places. One cannot tell if it is true, but I doubt it. Nothing very dangerous anyhow, mere scratches I should say, but in any case I have been spared the sight of him since then.

On the other hand, I believe it to be true that he had the impudence to wear the Princess' colors in the fray, which she is said to have chosen for him before we set out; that he flaunted them in his helm that morning, fighting in the sight of all men for his chosen lady. Thus, when he was warring so gallantly beneath the Prince's banner he was actually fighting for his beloved; when he saved the Prince's life he was still really fighting for her. And shortly before he had been in the arms of another woman, and presumably went straight from her couch to the battle, decking himself with the colors of his great passionate love! His true love blossomed like a wondrous flower above his chivalrously raised visor, while his body was still hot with the lust of betrayal. Certainly human love is a puzzle; it is small wonder that one cannot understand it.

Another puzzle is the relationship between these two men who are both bound to the same woman. Does that form the basis of a secret understanding? Sometimes it almost looks as if it did. Did Don Riccardo really save the Prince's life, as they say? I do not believe it, but he may have done so from sheer vanity, thus taking knightly revenge on the Prince who wished his death, and showing everybody what a magnanimous hero he is. That would be just like him. And did the Prince really mean to rescue Don Riccardo when he rode forward to help him in his mortal danger, although he had just been hoping he would die? I do not know. I cannot quite grasp it all. Surely one cannot hate and love a person at the same time?

I remember his expression that night, and it

boded death. But I also recall his moist dreaming eyes as he lay and listened to Don Riccardo discoursing on love, the great boundless love which fills us with its fire until our entire body is inflamed and consumed. Is love merely a beautiful poem containing nothing, at least nothing definite, but which everybody likes to listen to when it is well and feelingly recited? I do not know, but it is not quite impossible. These human beings are strange dissemblers.

I was also amazed at the Prince's behavior with the prostitute that night, for I had always held him to be above such things; not that it has anything to do with me, I am accustomed to his sudden transformations into someone quite different from what I had imagined. I mentioned it tactfully to a cameriere the next day, expressing my astonishment over what had happened, but he did not share my feelings. He said that the Prince always had mistresses, ladies of the court or the town, sometimes famous courtesans; just at present he favored the Princess' damigella, Fiammetta. He likes variety, explained the cameriere, laughing at me because I did not know it.

I cannot think how this can have escaped my customary acuteness. My uncritical admiration for my lord must have blinded me.

I do not care whether he has betrayed the Princess, for I hate her and ask nothing better than that she be betrayed. Besides, she is in love with Don Riccardo; it is to him that she addresses her glowing love letters, the ones which I have to carry next my heart. I sincerely hope he may be killed.

AT LAST it has stopped raining.

Today when we came out of the tent the sun shone brightly and the mountains rose in sharp outline around us, dripping with moisture, of course, and everywhere one heard the rushing of freshets which had not been there before. It was a crisp refreshing day; above, the sky was clear, and before us lay Montanza's old brigand city on its hill. We had almost forgotten what it looked like, but now one could distinguish every house within the walls and every arrow slit in the ancient keeps and even the small gilded crosses on the churches and belfries. Everything was much more clear-cut after the rain. Now it will not be long before the city is captured and finally obliterated from the face of the earth.

Everybody is very pleased at being able to come out into the fresh air, enlivened by the fine weather and longing for action. All discouragement and despondency have vanished and they are all anxious to fight again. I was mistaken when I thought that rain could spoil an army's morale. Its stupefying effect does not outlast its own duration.

There is life and movement in the tent lanes. The jesting soldiers polish their weapons, the squires rub their masters' armor till it shines, the horses are groomed and ridden to the watering places in the purling brooks which abound in the olive slopes, everybody is busy preparing for the coming battle. The camp is itself again, and the war has recovered the glamour and pageantry which so become it. Everything glitters in the sunlight—the soldiers in their gay accoutrements, the knights' armor and the gorgeous silver harness of the horses.

I have closely studied the town, the object of our campaign. It looks strong, almost impregnable, with its walls and fortresses, but we shall capture it, thanks not least to the valuable help contributed by Messer Bernardo. I have seen his new battering rams and catapults, his grappling irons and terrifying unsurpassed siege artillery: no fortress in the world can stand up against these. We shall smash our way through, blowing up and grinding everything to powder. We may even blast holes in the wall, using a subterranean passage in the way described that evening; we shall fight with every conceivable weapon, with everything that his great genius has created for us, and storm the town, spreading death and destruction as we pass through its streets. It will be burned and plundered and utterly obliterated from the face of the earth. Not one stone will be left upon another, and its population of pirates and brigands will at last receive their just punishment: they will be exterminated or taken away as prisoners and only smoking ruins will remain as a memorial of Montanza's erstwhile power and might. I am convinced that the Prince will crush his ancestral foes under an iron heel, and I dare not even think of how Boccarossa's men will conduct themselves. It will be our last, decisive triumph.

But first we must wipe out the forces which lie between us and the town. At a glance one can see that their number has been considerably increased, just as I foretold. Some say that it is an immense army, nearly as large as our own and Boccarossa's combined, but that is an exaggeration. It covers a much greater area than before, but to call it immense is to my mind to let oneself be unduly impressed by the enemy. The Prince's brow clouded somewhat at the first sight of it, but then he changed and seemed quite exhilarated as he watched it, patently rejoicing like a true soldier at the thought of the coming settlement of accounts and the long-awaited chance of a really good tussle. Not for one moment does he doubt our ultimate victory, nor, as far as I know, do any of his generals.

It will be delightful to take part in the storming of a city. Never before have I had such an opportunity.

I AM IN my usual seat in the dwarfs' apartment, and there, at the desk which forms part of the furnishings and which fits me very well and is very comfortable to write at, I shall continue with my memorandum of the strange and fateful happenings about me. This may sound unexpected, but a very simple explanation is forthcoming.

We won the battle. We knew it in advance, and also that it must involve considerable losses. The casualties on both sides were heavy, but presumably the enemy came off worse. In future it will be very difficult for them to put up any effective resistance, but for us also it was a serious bloodletting. The second day in particular was gory in the extreme. But what are soldiers for if not to be used? It was not nearly so bad as some maintain.

The reason for our presence here is that the Prince must return home to organize all his forces in order to bring the war to a victorious conclusion. And my inquiries have told me that it was also to obtain the requisite funds for the same object. Such an undertaking must consume huge sums of money. The Prince is said to be negotiating with the Venetian Signoria with a view to procuring them. Those hucksters have more than enough and soon the business will be settled. Then we shall take the field again.

They say that Boccarossa and his men have

asked for a higher wage and that they hold that they have not yet received their rights according to an earlier agreement. They are therefore making trouble about this. I had hardly expected them to attach so much importance to this aspect of the war, for none fight with such heroism and reckless- ness as they. I thought that they loved it for its own sake, as I do, but perhaps one cannot expect such selflessness. Maybe it is quite natural for them to want to be paid. All right, they will get their money.

There is also talk of other differences between them and the Prince—but there is so much talk. Some discontent is almost inevitable when an army has suffered losses and everything is not quite as it should be. Nobody is satisfied with the issue and each blames the other. Everybody is temporarily exhausted, they reckon up the casualties on either side and so on and so forth. And though there can be no doubt that Boccarossa's men are crazy about fighting, it is not because they want to further the Prince's great schemes, they may not think so much about *them*. But all these are transient matters of no consequence.

Besides, I am not sufficiently interested in all that and, least of all, in the economic trivialities connected with a thing like war, to wish to proceed with this subject. It will soon be settled.

It is dreadfully boring being at home again. Life

seems so meaningless, so utterly uneventful when one comes direct from the battlefield. Time drags on and one does not know what to do, all one's energy seems paralyzed. But it is only a matter of days and soon we shall go out again.

People here are very queer. I mean the servants and those who have not been at the war. They have no notion of what it is all about, it is as though they did not realize that the country is at war. They are surprised when they see me going about in armor, as though they did not know that such is the custom at the front. Were it otherwise one would be an easy prey to the enemy. It would be tantamount to exposing oneself to certain death. They say that there is no danger here, but there is a war going on just the same, and soon I shall be back in the thick of it. Any moment I expect the Prince's order to leave, and therefore I must be prepared for it. That is why I go about fully armed, but they cannot understand it.

They cannot imagine what the war is like, just because they have not taken any personal part in it. If one tries to give them a slight impression of martial life and its perils they look idiotically incredulous and fail to hide their secret envy. They try to make out that I have not experienced as much as I say, and have had no active share in the combats which I describe. It is easy to discover the envy which prompts them. No active share!

They do not know that my sword is still bloody in its sheath from the last engagement out yonder. I do not show it for I cannot endure the bragging which is so prevalent among soldiers, as exemplified by Don Riccardo. I merely lay my hand on the hilt of my sword and proceed calmly on my way.

Now it so happened that during the great two-day battle we were compelled to occupy a hill between our right wing and the town. It was a costly business but thereby our strategic position was greatly improved. Immediately afterward the Prince mounted the hill to reconnoiter the possibilities offered by this new conquest, and I followed him as a matter of course. On the summit was a pleasure house belonging to Lodovico, prettily situated and surrounded by cypresses and peach trees. Some soldiers and I searched the castle to see that there were no enemies ambushed there who might surprise us and threaten the person of the Prince, but we found only a pair of old servants. They were so feeble that they had been left behind and the Prince had given orders that they were not to be molested. Nevertheless, I went down to the cellar which nobody had thought of searching, but which might also have been used as a hiding place. There I found a dwarf who obviously belonged to Lodovico's court, for he keeps many dwarfs. He had also been left behind for some reason or other. The sight of me terrified him and he rushed into a dark passage. I cried: "Halt!" but he did not stop, so I understood that he could not have a clear conscience. I could not tell whether he was armed or not, so we had rather an exciting chase down the narrow twisting passages. At last he slipped into a room where there was an exit which he hoped to be able to use, but I was upon him before he could open the door. He realized that he was caught and wailed most lamentably. I hunted him along the walls like a rat, knowing that now he could not escape me, and at last I cornered him. I spitted him on my rapier and it pierced straight through him. He had no armor nor any of the customary battle equipment, only an absurd blue velvet jerkin with lace and fal-lals around the neck, just like a child. I left him lying there and returned to the daylight and the battle.

I do not relate this because I think it was anything extraordinary. It was but a trifle, such as may happen any day in wartime, and I do not boast about it; I simply did my duty as a soldier. Nobody knows anything about it, neither the Prince nor anyone else. None suspect that my rapier is dyed with blood and will remain so as a memory of my share, up to now, in the campaign.

In a way I am sorry that it was a dwarf I killed, for I would rather it had been one of the human beings whom I hate. Besides, the combat would have been even more exciting. But I hate my own people too, my own race is detestable to me. And during the fight, especially when dealing the death blow, I felt strangely exalted, as though I were performing a rite in an unfamiliar religion. It was the same when I throttled Jehoshaphat, an irresistible desire to destroy my own tribe. Why? I do not know. I cannot understand it. Is it my destiny thus to desire to exterminate my own race?

He had a piping castrato voice like all the dwarfs here, and that irritated me. My own voice is rich and deep.

It is a despicable and dishonored race.

Why are they not like me?

ToDAY the Princess tried to discuss love with me. She was very sentimental and lachrymose. Why, I don't know. But she certainly has reason to be—if she only knew how much! Then she suddenly switched over in her usual unaccountable way and began to jest about it instead. She sat in front of the mirror and the tiring woman arranged her hair while she passed from jest to earnest, chatting desultorily with me in a manner which I found both unwarranted and disagreeable. She was determined that I should make a statement on the subject, but I was not encouraging

She insisted: had I never had a little love affair?
I scowled and denied it stoutly. She was surprised
and incredulous and then she returned to the attack and became more and more inquisitive. At
last, wishing to forestall all further argument, I
declared that if ever I should love anybody it
would be a man.

She turned around and looked at me, laughing
heartily and the maid echoed her mirth. "A man!"
she cried provokingly, as though there were anything funny about it. "A man? Which one? Boccarossa maybe?" And they both went off again into
peals of laughter. I flushed, for I had been thinking of him, and when they marked my blushes
they seemed to think that added to the humor of
the whole thing.

I could see no humor in it, and I stared at them
with a frigid and contemptuous gaze. Laughter is
unlovely and disfiguring. Seeing their mouths suddenly open and uncover the red gums affects me
very unpleasantly. And I cannot help it if I cherish
a warm admiration, even a certain ardor for Boccarossa. In my eyes, he is a real man.

What particularly annoys me is that that slut of
a tiring wench should have laughed also, and so
much more coarsely than did Madama. I may
tolerate the Princess' poking fun at me, though at
any moment I could turn the jest to deadly earnest
and answer her question about love in the most

terrible way, telling her what it *really* is. I repeat that I can tolerate it from her, because she is my mistress and of princely blood, but that such a vulgar baggage should dare laugh at me—that enrages me. The trollop always has been insolent to me, trying to give herself airs and be "witty," and teasing me because I cannot open some of the palace doors. What has that got to do with her? She is a pert and clumsy peasant lass who ought to be whipped.

As for Boccarossa, it is quite natural that I should admire him; I, too, have a martial disposition.

THE DAYS pass, and we wait, not knowing what to do.

Yesterday I was sent with a message to Maestro Bernardo at Santa Croce. He is still there, working on his Last Supper. I have often wondered why he was not at the front, watching the crushing power of his own strange machines, but he seems content to construct them. I really thought that he would want to see them in action. Out there he could have had all the corpses he wanted to dissect and could have made great strides in his science.

I found him deep in contemplation of his noble creation, so preoccupied that he did not notice my entrance. When he raised his eyes they looked as though they were still very far away. He did not seem to pay much attention to my martial accouterment, though he never before had seen me so equipped. He noticed it, but showed neither surprise nor any special interest in it. "What do you want with me, little hobgoblin?" he asked amiably. I gave my message, though I was annoyed by his odd way of addressing me. Then I went away again, having no reason to stay. I threw a passing glance at the masterpiece, and thought that it did not seem nearer completion than when last I had seen it. He never finishes anything. What is it that he broods over all the time?

He never said a word about the war, though he could see that I had come straight from it. I had the impression that he was utterly indifferent to it.

The Signoria has refused to lend us any more money! Their envoy has announced that there will be no further loans. It is incredible! Absolutely incomprehensible! They think that the war has gone badly. Badly! What impertinence! *Badly!* When we have done nothing but win the whole time! We have penetrated far into enemy territory, right up to his capital. Now we are about to capture that, and harvest the fruits of our unique successes. To hinder us now! When the city lies there waiting to be taken, shot to pieces, burned, wiped off the face of the earth. It is outrageous! Unbelievable! Are those dirty hucksters to stand between us and our final victory? Just because they do not want to disburse their filthy money? No! It is not possible. That would be the lowest abomination!

The Prince must find a way out, and of course he will. A great and glorious war cannot be hampered by anything so vulgar as money! It is out of the question.

The palace is crammed with equerries, foreign envoys, councilors and commanders, and couriers spend their time shuttling between the Prince and the front.

I am absolutely crazy with excitement.

Boccarossa's mercenaries refuse to go on fighting! They want their pay, first that which is already due them, and double as much afterward. They will not stir until they have received this. The Prince cannot lay his hands on any money and he tries to coax them by pointing out that the city is a rich prize which, once captured, they will be free to plunder to their hearts' content. They reply that no one knows if the city ever will be captured, it has never happened before; first they must defeat il Toro's army and then start a long siege, and they do not like sieges, they find them boring. There is no chance of loot during a stationary siege. Besides, they have had severe losses, worse than they had expected, and this annoys them very much. They declare that, though they like killing, they have no wish to be killed, or at least not for such measly pay. There is no courtesy or diplomatic polish about their phraseology.

What is going to happen now? What will be the end of it all?

The Prince is sure to find some solution, his ingenuity is nothing short of devilish. He enjoys reverses, for they give him a chance to show his greatness. And our own invincible army still stands outside the walls of Montanza's capital. Let us not forget that!

The war is coming to an end! The troops are going to withdraw over the frontier and return home and everything is finished! Finished!

I must be dreaming! It must be a dream, a horrible nightmare! It cannot be true. I must wake up and find that it is only a dreadful detestable dream.

But it is true. *True!* Bitter unbelievable truth! All one's being refuses to grasp it.

Avarice, infamy, treachery, all human baseness combined has vanquished our heroic army and wrenched the weapons from its hands. Our glorious undefeated troops stand in their threatening might before the enemy's gates, yet they must retreat without exchanging a blow! They must go home, betrayed and abandoned, *home,* though their sole desire is to conquer or die! It is an outrageous, criminal tragedy.

Our great war, the noblest in all our history, to end like this!

I am stunned with pain and anger. Never in my life have I been so agitated nor suffered such shame. I am seething with bitterness, vexation and fury, and at the same time I am stunned, I feel utterly helpless. How can I influence the disgraceful course of events and how can I change it? How can I check the progress of this gloomy drama? I can do nothing. Nothing at all.

It is over. Everything is over. *Over!*

When I heard the news and finally grasped its import, I crept away to the dwarfs' apartment, so as to be alone with myself. I was afraid that my feelings might get the better of me, and that I should not be able to exercise manly self-control. Scarcely had I entered my little bare chamber when I began to shake all over in a paroxysm of sobs. I confess it: I could no longer hold it back. I pressed my clenched fists to my eyes in helpless fury and wept. *Wept!*

THE PRINCE keeps to his room, nor will he receive any visitors. He eats there in solitude. I wait on him and am the only one to see him except the servant who carries in the food. He seems quite calm, but it is not easy to say what may be hiding behind that pallid mask of his. His face is chalk white, framed in its black beard, his gaze immobile and unseeing. He scarcely notices my presence, and not a word passes his thin bloodless lips. The wretched servant is terrified of him, but then he is a miserable coward.

When he heard of the Venetian refusal, that the damned shopkeepers' republic intended to stop him from proceeding with the war, he flew into a passion such as I had never seen before. He literally foamed at the mouth with rage, a fearful sight. In his frenzy he seized his dagger and drove it into the table, nearly up to the hilt. If the despicable hucksters could have seen him then, I'll warrant they would have laid their money on the table without any further haggling.

A particular source of vexation is that he never had any real opportunity of utilizing Messer Bernardo's brilliant inventions. He would have been able to put them to good use, and he is convinced that with their aid we should have captured the city and that we were on the threshold of victory. But, if so, why did he not win it then?

It was a joy to witness his frenzy, but afterward I bethought me that perhaps he is not a very strong man. Why is he so dependent on others? Even on something so base and vile as money? Why did he not hurl our own unconquerable army against the

[118]

city and crush it? Are not armies meant for that?

I merely ask. I am no strategist, maybe I do not understand the art of war, but my soul too is filled with pain and wonder over our incomprehensible fate.

I have unbuckled my armor. In sorrow and vexation I have put it aside in the dwarfs' apartment. It hangs there as helplessly as a miserable jumping jack on its nail. Humiliated. Dishonored.

We HAVE been at peace for nearly four weeks now. The palace, the town and the whole country are wrapped in gloom. It is strange how depression and uneasiness can spread themselves abroad during a prolonged peace. One knows exactly what it is going to feel like; the air begins to thicken and exude that stagnant suffocating vapidity which is so depressing to the senses; the returning soldiers are discontented, nothing suits them, and the stay-at-homes are irritable and snappish with them, perhaps because the war has not had the desired result. Daily life continues its sluggish futile aimless course. All the hopefulness and gaiety of the war have been swept away.

The court is moribund. Nobody passes through the main gate, except those of us who reside here, and we generally use one of the other entrances. There are no visitors from abroad, no guests are announced and none are invited. The halls are deserted and even the courtiers keep in the background. One seldom meets a soul in the empty corridors and the stairways echo beneath one's solitary feet. It is almost uncanny, like an abandoned castle. And within, in his secluded chamber, the Prince strides up and down or sits brooding at his table, where the hole from his dagger blade gapes like an open wound. He sits glaring ahead of him, pondering over God knows what.

It is a gloomy depressing time. The day drags itself painfully along until at last it is evening again.

I have more than enough time to write my notes on my experiences and my meditations, but I have no energy at all. I spend most of my time sitting at the window, watching the sluggish gray-yellow river flowing outside the castle wall, staining it a bilious green.

The river which once upon a time witnessed our glorious victories in the land of il Toro!

No, no, this is monstrous! It is more upsetting than anything else which has happened during this terrible time! The earth reels beneath my feet and I have no more faith in anything under the sun!

Is it conceivable—the Prince thinks that he and

the house of Montanza should make friends and sign a pact never to make war on each other again! They are going to stop this perpetual fighting and solemnly bind themselves to put an end to it forever. Never again will they draw their swords against each other! It seems that, to begin with, il Toro refused, presumably in annoyance because he had been recently attacked, but the Prince continued even more earnestly to urge his proposition. Why should our two people go on destroying each other, what is the use of all these meaningless wars? They have been going on intermittently for two centuries, and neither has been able definitely to defeat the other, so that both have been the losers in this eternal warfare. It has brought us nothing but famine and misery. How much better it would be if we could live in peace and mutual understanding, so that our countries could flourish and rejoice as they should have done from the beginning. Lodovico is reported to have begun to pay heed to the Prince's proposals and found them reasonable. Now he has answered that he is of the same mind and has accepted an invitation to negotiate this lasting peace and sign the solemn treaty.

I think the world has gone mad! Lasting peace! No more war! What flummery, what childishness! Do they think they can change the cosmic system? What conceit! And what infidelity toward the past and the great traditions! No more war! Is there to be no more bloodshed, and are glory and honor to be of no further account? Will the silver bugle never blow again as the knights charge with their lances in rest? Will the troops never clash again and meet their heroic death on the field of battle? And then will there be nothing left to put a limit to the bottomless pride and arrogance of mankind? No Boccarossa with his broadsword, pock-marked and close-lipped, to show these people the powers that reign over them? Are the very foundations of life to be dislocated?

Reconciliation! Could anything be more shameful? Reconciliation with a mortal enemy! What perversity, what warped and repulsive artifice! And what degradation, what humiliation, for us, our army, our dead! What dishonor for our fallen heroes whose sacrifice was in vain. It is nauseatingly horrible!

So *that* was what he was meditating. I often wondered what it might be—and that is what it was! And now he is in a better temper, he has begun to talk again as usual, and seems quite lively and pleased with himself. I suppose he thinks he has had a brilliant inspiration, a really great idea.

There are no words for my contempt. My faith in my lord, the Prince, has suffered a jar from which it cannot recover. He has sunk as deeply as any prince can. Eternal peace! Eternal armistice!

No more wars in all eternity! Only peace, peace! Truly it is not easy to be the dwarf of such a lord.

THE WHOLE palace is upside down, thanks to this idiotic entertainment. One stumbles over brooms and pails, there are mounds of rubbish everywhere, whose dust clogs one's throat when they are shoveled out of the windows. They have taken ancient tapestries down from the attic and rolled them out on the floor so that one treads on the sheepish love scenes; later they will be suspended on the walls to beautify this shameful "feast of peace and concord." Guest apartments which had not been used for years have been put to rights again, and the servants run about like half-wits, scuttling to and fro in order to get everything done in time. This imbecile scheme of the Prince's displeases them all, and besides, it involves so much toil and effort. They are doing up the Palazzo Geraldi, for it too will be occupied: Lodovico's escort is going to be quartered there. They say it looks like a pigsty after Boccarossa's stay. The larders are crammed with food, hundreds of oxen, calves and sheep, which the castellan has forced the wretched people to deliver, as well as grain and forage. They are, of course, annoyed, and the whole country is seething with discontent.

I believe that, if they could, they would rebel against the Prince thanks to his stupid notion of a "peace feast." Deer are slain in the parks, pheasants and hare are trapped and shot, and the boars are hunted in the mountains. The falconers come to the kitchen with their quails, partridges, and herons, pigeons are slaughtered, the capons in the coops are tested for their fat, and peacocks are selected for the great gala banquet which is to take place one of these days. The tailors are making costly attire for the Prince and Princess and all the patricians in the town, garments of rare materials from Venice—*they* can be had on credit, but none is given for the war. They fit and try on and go rushing in and out of the palace. Triumphal arches are being erected outside the castle and down the street where Lodovico and his train will pass. Baldachins are set up in front of the palace gate and inside the hall, and they are busy brushing and beating the carpets which are going to hang from the windows. The musicians drive one mad practicing their pieces all day long, and the court poets scribble some nonsense which is going to be recited in the great throne room. Nothing but preparations for this idiotic feast! It is the sole topic of conversation, nobody gives a thought to anything else. The whole court is in a turmoil and every corner is in disorder; one cannot take a step without getting in somebody's way or stumbling over something; everything is in an indescribable muddle.

I am so furious, I could burst.

THE ENEMY has made his solemn entry into our capital, which was decorated in his honor as it never has been before. Lodovico Montanza and his whippersnapper of a son, Giovanni, rode through the streets, preceded by thirty mounted trumpeters and flutists, surrounded by a body-guard of green-and-black-clad cavalry with their partisans in rest, and followed by a choice company of knights and nobles. Last came two hundred archers, also on horseback. Lodovico rode a black stallion, saddled in dark green velvet with silver embroideries and silver harness, and everywhere the people acclaimed him, as they always do at the word of command, irrespective of the object of their cheers. Now they pretend to themselves that they are delighted at the prospect of eternal peace. The Prince had sent three heralds to meet him and these proclaimed his arrival and the reason for his visit, and all the church bells began to ring. Our degradation could not have had a more brilliant inauguration. They even gave a salute from the moats with culverins firing up into the empty sky, but to my mind they should have been aimed at the arrivals and loaded with live ammunition. The princeling's horse was scared by these or something else, and it seemed as though he might fall off, but he soon resumed control of his mount and rode on, rather red in the face. He looks childish and cannot be more than seventeen. Though the mishap was avoided, it made the people wonder whether it might not be an evil omen. They are always on the lookout for omens on these solemn occasions and this was the only incident which gave them anything to whet their wits on.

Lodovico alighted from his horse before the palace gate and was welcomed by the Prince with grandiloquent phrases. He is a little stocky man with fat smooth cheeks so sanguine as to be streaked with red and a short thick bull neck. His scanty beard grows low on his cheeks and is scarcely an ornament to his otherwise comely face. The keen gray eyes try to look friendly, but that is nothing to go by, for we all know him to be a scoundrel He seems choleric and as if he might have a stroke at any moment.

The day has been filled with reception ceremonies, meals, and negotiations about the pact between the two states, discussing its wonderful clauses and final wording. This evening there was an appallingly boring theatrical performance in Latin, of which I did not understand a word, nor did anybody else as far as I could see. But afterward they presented a scabrous comedy, in everyday language, which everyone appreciated. They all reveled in its vulgarities and numerous obscenities. I found it disgusting.

Now at last the day has come to an end, and I sit alone here in my chamber and am grateful for my solitude. Nothing gives me such satisfaction as being alone. Luckily the ceiling is very low in the dwarfs' apartment. Otherwise, they might have lodged some of the guests here, and that would have been frightful.

That princeling is considered handsome, I imagine, but in that case he has not inherited his looks from his father. When he came riding alongside the latter, on his horse with its blue velvet trappings and dressed to match, people declared that he was good-looking. It is possible, but I find him far too delicate and unmanly with his hind's eyes, his long black hair and the sensitive skin which colors up for no reason. It may be my fault, but I cannot bring myself to appreciate that kind of looks. To my mind, a man should look like a man. They say he resembles his mother, the fair and much eulogized Beatrice, who was very beautiful, and is said to be already in paradise although it is only ten years since she died.

This afternoon I saw him walking with Angelica in the rose garden, and a little later in the day they went down to the river and fed the swans with bread crumbs. On both occasions I could see that they were talking to each other. I cannot understand what he could have to say to such a stupid child, nor can he have seen how plain she is, or he would have avoided her company. Perhaps he is as foolish as she.

Naturally Don Riccardo takes part in all the ceremonies, pushing himself forward on every possible occasion. His wounds are already healed. What did I say? There is no sign of them, except one arm is a little stiff. So much for his heroism!

THIS IS the third day since the enemy came into the town. The festivities in his honor continue without a break and one never has a moment's peace. I was too tired last night to make any notes and am writing this morning instead, just a few lines about the happenings of the day and my impressions thereof. The two princes left the castle before dawn and spent several hours hawking on the meadows to the west of the town. Lodovico is very much interested in the sport, and the Prince has a fine collection of falcons, including some rare birds which were presented to him by the King of France, and whose prowess he likes to demonstrate. Then they ate for hours, and there was a concert to which we were forced to listen, though I know of nothing more detestable than music. Afterward, we had Moorish dancing and music and some jugglers who aroused much admiration and were the only thing worth seeing. Immediately after this they started eating again, and went on until late at night, when a shameless masque was presented with men and women in such close-fitting garments that they seemed almost naked. By that time most of them were dead drunk. At last the day's program was completed, and I was able to go to bed, where I fell asleep, utterly exhausted.

All this time, the Prince is in the highest good humor, amiable and charming as never before. He cannot do enough for his "guests," and truckles to them in the most sickening manner. It revolts me to see him. He and il Toro are like intimate friends; at least he seems to be a sincere friend. At the beginning, Lodovico was somewhat reserved and perhaps a thought suspicious, but all that has disappeared now. He came here with a strong bodyguard and a force of several hundred men. One wonders if so many warriors are necessary for the signing of a lasting peace, but such is the custom. And a prince cannot appear at a foreign court without a large train. I have all the customs at my fingertips, but I cannot bear to sit quiescent and see all these enemies around me.

I cannot understand my lord's behavior—how can he conduct himself so disgracefully toward our archenemies? I am utterly at a loss, but that is nothing unusual; it is my destiny never to understand this man. However I do not want to dwell on it any longer, but shall merely repeat what I have said before: that my contempt for him knows no bounds.

Yesterday Giovanni and Angelica were together again more than once, apparently very bored. I saw them sitting by the river in the twilight, but this time they did not feed the swans nor did they speak to each other. They sat silently side by side watching the river flow by. They can have nothing more to say to each other.

What else is there to write about? There was nothing else. Today the peace pact is going to be solemnly signed, and then comes the great banquet with its various pastimes which will last far into the night. I am very depressed and unutterably bored with everything.

The Prince has confided in me—something so glorious that it makes the brain reel: I cannot breathe a word about it; it is a secret between the two of us. Never before have I realized how closely we are bound together.

All I can say is that I am tremendously happy.

The gala banquet begins at six this evening. It is to be the climax of the festivities, and such extensive preparations have been made for it that it cannot fail to be a success. I feel as though I were about to explode.

He is a great Prince!

Now I shall relate the story of yesterday and, above all, I shall describe the great feast which concluded the peace ceremonies connected with the treaty between our princely house and that of Montanza; and what happened there.

First we assembled in the throne room and the treaty of lasting peace between our states was read aloud. Its wording was eloquent and high-sounding, and it also contained clauses relative to the abolishment of the border fortresses and free trade between our peoples and various agreements to facilitate this trade. Then came the signatures. The princes stepped forward to the table, followed by their chief nobles, and put their names on the two large documents which lay there. It was quite impressive. There followed a blaring fanfare from sixty trumpeters who stood along the four walls of the hall, at a distance of three paces from each other, clad alternately in our own and Montanza's colors. Then those present trooped into the great banqueting hall with the master of ceremonies at their head, to the festal strains of specially composed music. The mighty room was lighted by fifty silver candelabra and two hundred torches held by lackeys in gilded liveries and also by lads who had been taken straight from the streets, dressed in foul rags with their bare dirty feet on the stone floor. At close quarters they smelled very disagreeable. There were five tables in the hall, weighed down with silver and majolica and vast dishes of cold meats and fruit of every hue, and twenty large groups of statuary modeled in sponge cake, which they told me represented various scenes from Greek mythology, a heathen faith of which I know little. All the appointments in the middle of the central table were of gold—candelabra, fruit bowls, plates, wine ewers and goblets—and here sat both the princes and all the other persons of royal blood and our and Montanza's chiefest followers. The Prince sat opposite il Toro and beside him was the Princess in a gown of crimson with slashed jeweled sleeves of white damask and heavy gold embroideries over her fat bosom. On her head she wore a silver net studded with diamonds which flattered her ugly chestnut hair and, since she had indubitably spent several hours painting herself, it was for once easy to see that her plump flabby face must one time have been very beautiful. She smiled her own special smile. The Prince wore a simple close-fitting suit of black velvet, the sleeves inset with pleated yellow silk. He was slim and youthful and supple as a rapier. He was rather reserved, but seemed to be in good humor, for time

[132]

and again he stroked his short black hair as is his habit when pleased. I felt passionately devoted to him. Il Toro was clad in a short, very broad-shouldered coat of dark green cloth and rare sables, and beneath that a scarlet suit with heavy golden chains depending from the collar. In this garb he looked shorter and burlier than ever, and his thick bull neck protruded from the brown sable fur in all its crimson obstinacy. In appearance he was well-bred amiability personified, but one cannot judge by people's faces. It is their bodies which show them as the kind of animals they are.

Of course Don Riccardo was at that part of the table, in one of the best places, though by rights he should have been sitting at one of the other tables. He always pushes himself forward and naturally the Prince cannot do without him—nor the Princess either for that matter. He chattered and showed off from the very beginning, twiddling contentedly at his curly black beard. I gave him an icy glance, which none but myself could interpret. But enough of that.

A little apart—though how could that be, since they too were sitting at the table like all the others —were Giovanni and Angelica, side by side. It was natural that they should have been placed together since they were of much the same age and both of princely blood. At least he is, but she may very well be a bastard. They were the only young things among the many hundred guests and they seemed more like children than adults, and therefore rather apart from the others. It looked almost as though they had come there by mistake. Poor Angelica was making her entry into the great world and was dressed up in a white satin gown with long tight-fitting sleeves of gold brocade and a coif of pearls and thin gold thread on her colorless fair hair. Of course she looked frightful, and for those who were accustomed to seeing her in plain almost common clothes, the effect was grotesque and pretentious. Her mouth was agape as usual and the baby cheeks red with shyness. Her big blue eyes shone as though they had never seen so much as a wax candle before. Giovanni, too, seemed rather embarrassed among all these people and kept throwing them bashful glances, but he was a trifle more sophisticated, and the bashfulness appeared more to be a part of his nature. He was dressed in blue velvet with a gold embroidered collar and a narrow chain with an oval gold locket which is reported to contain a portrait of his mother, she whom they say is in paradise—but who can tell? She may just as well be writhing in purgatory. He is deemed handsome. I heard some of the guests whisper something about it, but when I then heard them talking about a "handsome couple" I realized that they must have a very peculiar notion of beauty. At any rate he is not to my taste. I think that a man should look like a man. One cannot believe that he is a prince and a Montanza. How will he ever be able to reign over a people and sit on a throne? Personally, I doubt if he will ever get a chance to do so.

The children took no part in the conversation and seemed grievously embarrassed when anyone looked at them. Nor did they talk very much together, but I noticed how they kept looking strangely at each other, and smiling secretly whenever their eyes met. I was surprised to see the girl smile, for as far as I remember I have never seen her do so before, at least not since she was quite small. She smiled very carefully as though feeling her way. Perhaps she knew that her smile was not beautiful. But then I never think that human beings are beautiful when they smile.

After closely watching their behavior I began to wonder more and more what might be the matter with them. They scarcely touched their food and at times they just sat there staring down at their plates. I could see that their hands were meeting in secret under the table. When anybody near by leaned against his neighbor and observed them, they became bewildered and red in the face and began to talk very earnestly to each other. By degrees I realized that there was something special between them—that they were in love with each other. This discovery had a strange effect on me. I scarcely know why it upset me so much, and made such a disagreeable impression on me.

Love is always disgusting, but love between these two who were no more than a pair of innocent children, seemed to me more repulsive than anything I had previously known. The mere sight of it made me burn with wrath and indignation.

But more of this later. I have dallied far too long with these infants who, after all, were not the principal figures at the banquet. I shall continue with my description of the latter.

After the guests had eaten the cold meats of which there was a profusion on the tables, the major-domo appeared in the doorway, mounted on a white mare saddled in purple, and loudly announced the first twelve dishes which were then borne in by numerous camerieri and scalchi, to the strains of a fanfare blown by two trumpeters who led the mare by the bridle. The smoking dishes spread a smell of meat, sauces, and fat which impregnated the whole room, and I, who can hardly endure the stink of food, was within an ace of vomiting. The seneschal arched his back like a cockerel and strutted importantly to the Prince's table, where he began to carve the roasts, ducks and capons, the grease dripping from the fingers of his left hand which held the viands. All the while, he gesticulated with the long carving knife which he held in his right hand, as though he were a famous fencer exhibiting his perilous art. The guests stuffed themselves with food and I began to feel the discomfort, the vague nausea from which I always suffer when I see people eating, especially when they are gluttonous. They gaped in the most disgusting manner in order to make room for the too large bits and their jaw muscles champed in constant unison, while one could see the tongue moving about the food inside the mouth. Il Toro was the unpleasantest of all those who sat at the Prince's table. He ate like a churl, devouring everything with a shocking appetite, and he had a nasty bright scarlet tongue, broad like that of an ox. On the other hand, the Prince did not eat voraciously. He partook of less than usual that evening and scarcely drank at all. Once I saw him raise his glass to himself and, sunk deep in thought, gaze into its greenish depths as though surveying the world through them. The others drank tremendously. The servants kept running around and filling up the goblets and beakers.

Gilded sturgeon, carp and pike were borne in on immense majolica dishes, receiving great applause for their skillful dressing, mighty galantines adorned with wax ornaments so that one could not see what they really were, pasties shaped like the heads of deer and calves, sucking pigs roasted whole and gilded, and sugared and perfumed dishes composed of fowls, quails, pheasants and herons. At last came two pages clad as hunters carrying an entire wild boar, as gilded as the rest, with flames issuing from its jaws which had been filled with a burning substance that smelled most foully. Girls dressed, or rather undressed, as nymphs, ran in to strew the floor with scented powders, in order to get rid of the disgusting stench, but the result was worse than ever, and the air became suffocatingly stuffy. For a space, I could scarcely breathe.

Il Toro accepted a portion of the boar as though he had eaten nothing before, and all the others took huge slices of the dark red flesh which still dripped blood, but was, nevertheless, regarded as a delicacy. It was horrible to see them start their chewing again, while the gravy trickled from their lips and beards; there was something shameless about the spectacle, and I who always avoid eating in public and never consume more than is absolutely necessary to maintain life, was more and more nauseated by these red swollen oversized creatures who seemed to be all stomach. Then, too, it was horrible to see the boar being opened up by the seneschal and the gory slices cut out of its inside until at last only the skeleton and a few rags of flesh remained.

Don Riccardo, eating left-handedly and with a special servant to cut his meat for him, put away a large quantity and drank deeply. His face was one wide foolish smile, and with his good arm he kept raising his goblet to his lips. His outfit of dark red velvet was meant to personify some kind of passion—he always dresses himself for his mistress. His eyes were brighter and wilder than usual and every now and again he gesticulated and recited some nonsensical poem or other, addressing anybody who would listen to him, except the Princess. High-sounding words about love and the joy of living flowed out of him as soon as the wine had poured down his throat. The Princess' eyes glistened whenever he looked at her, and she smiled her mysterious smile at him. Otherwise, she sat there as usual during a feast, half present and half absent. Sometimes they glanced sideways at each other when they thought nobody else was looking, and then her eyes shone with a moist, almost morbid, luster. I noticed them. I never let them out of my sight, though they had no notions of it. Nor did they guess what was brewing in my soul. Who knows anything of that? Who knows what I, the dwarf, have abrewing in my innermost being, to which none has access? Who knows anything about the dwarf soul, the most enclosed of all, where their fate is determined? Who can guess my true identity? It is well for them that they cannot, for if they did they would be terrified. If they did, the smile would die on their faces and their lips would wither and fade forever. Not all the wine in the world would make them red and moist again.

Is there no wine in the world can make them moist again? Will they never smile again?

I also looked at the damigella Fiammetta who, though not at the Prince's table, was quite honorably placed, better than her position warranted. She is fairly new to the court, and I had not paid much attention to her before, though I cannot think why. In point of fact, she is startingly handsome, tall and straight, young and yet mature, ripe for the world. Her face is dark and hard and very proud, with pure regular features and coal-black eyes with a deep-lying glint in them. I noticed that the Prince sometimes cast an uneasy glance in her direction, as though trying to discover what was going on behind her immobile face, or guess at her thoughts or mood. She never looked at him.

Now nearly all the lights in the hall were extinguished and a titillating music was heard, though no one knew its source. Twelve Moorish dancers came rushing into the darkness with burning torches between their teeth, and began to perform a mad breath-taking dance. Now they whirled with a ring of fire around their black heads, now they brandished their torches in the air or flung them high and caught them again between their glittering fangs. They played with the fire as though with something dangerous, and everybody stared at them, half fascinated and half scared by their strange demoniac appearance. They swarmed about the place where the princes were sitting and when they flourished their torches the sparks showered over the table. Their dusky faces were twisted into fierce grimaces as they lit the torches, and they resembled spirits of the underworld whence they had brought their fire. And why should they not have lighted them there? Why should they not have dipped their torches in the flames of hell? I stood with my old dwarf's face hidden in the darkness and watched these spirits and their strange demoniac dance which seemed to have had the devil for teacher.

And as though to indicate their origin and recall the kingdom of death to which all must one day return, they ended by turning down their torches and extinguishing them on the floor; then they vanished as though the earth had opened and engulfed them.

There was a grisly feeling in the air before the lights went up again, and my dwarf's eyes, which see better in the dark than the eyes of men, observed that some of the guests sat with their hands on their dagger hilts, as though ready for anything.

Why? It was only a troupe of dancers which the Prince had hired in Venice to entertain his guests.

The hall was illuminated again and immediately

the major-domo reappeared in the doorway on his white mare and, to the shrill strains of a fanfare, announced the most exquisite course of the evening: *"Pavoni!"* Whereupon fifty servitors hastened in from every side, bearing aloft huge jeweled silver dishes on which were enthroned as many peacocks, gilded and with their iridescent tails outspread. Everybody manifested the most idiotic delight at the sight, and the depression aroused by the down-turned torches, presaging death, was swept away. These creatures are like children, forgetting one game for another. But they never forget the game I play with them.

Having gaped their fill at the monstrous dishes, they proceeded to devour them, just as they had done with all the other victuals. The banquet began all over again with the appearance of these vainglorious birds which I have always detested and which remind me of human beings, but that may be the reason why men admire them so and regard them as a delicacy. As soon as they had been gobbled up, new courses were brought in, pheasants, capons, quails, and ducks again, sturgeon, carp, and dripping venison steaks, fresh quantities of food with which they stuffed themselves until my mounting disgust was turned to nausea. Then came mounds of cakes, confectionery, and sweetmeats stinking of musk, which they swallowed as though they had had nothing else to eat throughout the evening. And at last they flung themselves upon the groups of Greek mythological statuary which they had pronounced so rarely beautiful and cut them up and devoured them until only a few morsels remained, and the stained tables looked as though they had been devastated by a horde of barbarians. I looked at the havoc and the hot sweaty creatures with the greatest aversion.

Now the master of ceremonies stepped forward and requested silence. He announced the performance of a superlatively beautiful allegory, composed at the Prince's gracious command by his court poets for the diversion and edification of the honored guests. The skinny sallow scribblers who sat far down at the humblest table pricked up their ears and looked stupider than ever as they eagerly and superciliously awaited the performance of their work of genius, whose profound and symbolic purport was to constitute the climax of the feast.

Mars made his entrance on a stage at one side of the hall, clad in shining armor, and declared that he had decided to compel the two mighty champions Celefon and Kalixtes to a combat which should be renowned throughout the world and crown their names with eternal glory, but above all would tell mankind the power and the glory of himself, the god of war, how at his command gallant blood would flow and heroes fight each other at his will. He concluded by saying that as long as courage and chivalry remained on earth they would be at the service of Mars and none other, and then left the scene.

Now appeared the two champions and as soon as they caught sight of each other they began their sparring, so that their blades flashed through the air, and there followed a lengthy bout of fencing which was much appreciated by those in the hall who understood its subtleties. Even I must admit that they were notable swordsmen and I took great pleasure in that part of the piece. During the duel they pretended to inflict grievous wounds on each other and staggered exhaustedly under them until they sank lifeless to the floor.

The god of war reappeared and perorated about the honorable combat which had caused their heroic deaths, about his irresistible power over the senses of men and about himself, the mightiest on earth of all the Olympic gods.

After his departure a gentle music was heard. Shortly afterward the goddess Venus glided in, followed by her attendants, and found the two knights sadly mangled and, as she herself said, bathing in their blood. The attendant nymphs bent over them, lamenting that two such fine handsome men should have been needlessly bereft of their manhood and should have ceased to breathe. As

they wept over this tragic fate, their mistress declared that only the cruel Mars could have incited
them to this senseless duel. To this the nymphs
agreed, but reminded her that Mars had once been
her lover and that despite her celestial gentleness
she had held him in her arms. But she asserted that
this was a base slander, for how could the goddess
of love favor the wild and barbaric deity who was
hated and shunned by all, including his own father,
the great Jupiter? Then she stepped forward and
touched the fallen champions with her magic
wand, whereupon they rose up all hale and hearty
and pressed each other's hands in token of lasting
peace and friendship, swearing that never again
would they yield to the fearsome Mars and wage
bloody war against each other.

Then the goddess made a long and moving
speech about love, praising it as the strongest and
gentlest of all powers, as the source and vivifying
origin of all things; of its delicate might which
imbues strength with gentleness, which dictates
heavenly laws for earthly beings, and compels all
living creatures to obey them; which can change
and purify the hard coarse senses of men, the acts
of princes and customs of the people; of brotherly
love and charity reigning in a devastated and
bloodstained world with chivalry and magnanim-
ity in their service, bestowing other virtues on mankind than those of martial glory and feats of arms.

Raising her magic wand she proclaimed that her almighty divinity would conquer the earth and transform it into the happy abode of love and eternal peace.

If my face had been able to smile I should have done so during this ingenuous epilogue, but these sentimental outpourings were most flatteringly received and caused many of those present to feel really moved and enchanted, so that the last mellifluous words were followed by an almost reverential silence. The scribblers who had achieved this result looked highly pleased and obviously appropriated to themselves all the credit of this successful entertainment, although nobody gave them a thought. Undoubtedly they regarded this eloquent and skillful allegory as the only important item in all the festivities which celebrated the peace treaty between our princely house and that of Montanza. But I wonder if what was to follow was not the most important of all.

As usual I had my place behind my princely lord, and from the depths of my experience could guess at his wishes before they were uttered, sometimes before he even formulated them to himself, thus fulfilling his commands as though I were a part of himself. Now he gave me a sign, imperceptible to all others, which meant that I was to serve il Toro, his son, and his foremost men with the rare wine which is in my sole keeping and

which I alone know how to prepare. I fetched my
golden ewer and filled il Toro's goblet. He had
thrown off his fur-trimmed coat which had become
too warm during all his potations, and there he sat
in his scarlet garb, short and stout and sanguine,
his face as red as fire. The golden chains round his
bull neck were tangled together so that he looked
as if he were fettered in them. I filled his goblet to
the brim. His replete body exuded an odor of
sweat, eructations and wine fumes, and it nearly
made me vomit to be so near such a repulsive
bestial creature. I thought: "Is there anything so
vile as a human being?" and continued down the
table to some of his foremost men, commanders
and noble lords, who had been put at the Prince's
table. Then I filled Giovanni's gold beaker, while
Angelica looked at me with her stupid bright blue
eyes, as foolish and wondering as in her childhood
days when she read in my compressed old man's
face that I did not want to play with her. I saw
that she dropped his hand when I approached and
I also saw how she paled, presumably because she
feared that I had discovered their shameful secret.
And she was quite right. With disgust I had observed their growing intimacy, the more shameful
since they belonged to two opposing parties, and
were themselves but innocent children who had
allowed themselves to be dragged down into the
slough of love. I had observed their blushes, caused

by the fire of love within their veins, by concu-
piscent appetites whose revelation is enough to
make one sick. It was with the strongest distaste
that I had marked the combination of innocence
and carnal desires which is particularly nauseating
and whereby love between persons of that age is
rendered even viler and more abhorrent than any
other kind. I took pleasure in filling his beaker
which was only half empty, but that is of no consequence when I add my own wine.

Last of all I approached Don Riccardo and
filled his goblet to the brim. It was not part of my
mission, but I have missions of my own. I give
myself orders to fulfill. When I saw the Prince
looking at me I met his eyes with serenity. They
were strange. Human eyes are sometimes like that
—a dwarf's never. It was as though everything in
his soul had floated to the surface and was watching me and my actions with mingled fear, anxiety, and desire; as though strange monsters had
emerged from the depths, twisting and turning
with their slimy bodies. An ancient being like myself never looks like that. I stared straight in his
eyes and I hope that he noticed the steadiness of
my hand.

I know what he wants, but I also know that he
is a knight. I am no knight, but only the dwarf of
a knight. I can guess his desires before they have
been uttered, perhaps before he has formulated

them to himself, and thus I perform his most inaudible commands, as though I were a part of himself. It is good to have a little bravo like that who can render all manner of service.

While I filled Don Riccardo's goblet, which was empty as usual, he leaned back guffawing with laughter so that his beard stood straight out and his mouth with all its broad white teeth gaped open like a crater. I could see right down his throat. I have already mentioned my distaste for laughing people, but the sight of this fool who "loves life" and finds it so irresistibly amusing, roaring with vulgar laughter, was particularly revolting. His gums and lips were wet and the tears swam in the nasty little glands in the corners of his eyes from which radiated small red streaks over the dark brown unnaturally brilliant eyes. His larynx bounced up and down under the short black bristles on his throat. On his left hand he wore a ruby ring which I recognized as one which the Princess had given him when he was ill and which I had carried next my heart wrapped up in one of her nauseous love letters. Everything about him disgusted me.

I do not know what he was laughing at, nor does it matter, for I certainly should not have found it in the least amusing. Anyhow he never did so again.

My task was done. I awaited further developments beside this ebullient fool of a whoremonger, and smelt the stink of him and the velvet of his dark red suit which was meant to express passion.

My lord the Prince raised his greenish goblet, turning his amiable smile toward the honored guests, toward Lodovico Montanza and his brilliant train around the table, but most of all toward il Toro who was sitting opposite him. His pale aristocratic face was delicate and noble and very different from the hot and swollen countenances of the others. In gentle but virile tones he bade them drink a toast to the lasting peace which henceforth should reign between their two states, between the princely houses and between the peoples. The long meaningless fighting was at an end and a new era had started which was going to bring peace and prosperity to us all. The old saying of peace on earth was at last to be realized. Thereupon he drained his glass and in solemn silence the noble guests emptied their golden goblets.

Afterward my lord remained sitting with his glass in his hand and his absent gaze seemed to be contemplating the world through it.

The ripple of voices began again and I do not know exactly how long it lasted; that kind of thing is difficult to reckon, one loses a sense of time. I was far too strung up, violently and indescribably so, and furious because Giovanni had not touched his wine. Aflame with wrath I saw Angelica smile faintly and pull it toward her, pretending that she wanted to drink it herself. I had hoped that they would both do so, that in their infatuation they would want to drink from the same source; but neither touched it. Perhaps the accursed girl suspected something, perhaps in their prurient exaltation they felt no need of wine. I seethed with bitterness. Why should they live? Devil take them!

Don Riccardo on the other hand gulped it down in a single draught. He emptied this his last goblet to the Princess, saluting the "lady of his heart" as usual. In a last attempt at wit he gesticulated humorously with his useless right arm and raised the excellent libation which I had served him with his left hand, smiling the while that much admired but essentially vulgar smile of his. And she smiled back at him, first rather mischievously, and then with that moist desirous glint in her eyes which I find so sickening. I cannot understand how anybody can have that kind of expression in his eyes.

Suddenly il Toro gave vent to a weird howl and stared straight ahead of him with stiff glaring eyes. Two of his men who had been sitting on the same side of the Prince's table hastened to him, but simultaneously began to stagger, seized the edge of the table and collapsed on their seats, where they writhed in agony, groaning something about having been poisoned. Not many heard them, but one of the others, who was not yet so seriously affected, shouted to the whole room: "We are poisoned!" Everybody sprang up and confusion reigned. Other members of il Toro's suite leaped up with drawn daggers and other weapons and rushed to the central table where they attacked our men and tried to push their way through to the Prince. But his followers had risen in their turn to defend themselves and their lord, and a terrible tumult began. There were many killed and wounded on both sides and blood flowed in torrents. It was like a battlefield indoors among the decked tables, between drunken red-faced warriors who after sitting peacefully beside each other suddenly found themselves fighting desperately for their lives. Screams echoed from every side and drowned the groans and sighs of the dying. Appalling curses summoned all the devils in hell to this spot where the foulest of all crimes had been committed. I climbed onto a chair so as to get a good view of what was happening about me and stood there, frenzied with excitement, surveying the tremendous results of my work: the extirpation by me of this loathsome race which deserves nothing else. I saw how my mighty sword went forth over them, pitilessly destructive, demanding vengeance and punishment for everything. How I dispatched them to burn eternally in the fires of hell! May they burn forever! All these creatures who call themselves men, and who inspire such disgust and nausea! Why should they exist? Why should they revel and laugh and love and overrun the earth? Why should these lying dissemblers and braggarts exist, these lustful shameless creatures whose virtues are even viler than their sins? May they burn in the fires of hell! I felt like Satan himself, surrounded by all the infernal spirits invoked at their nocturnal meetings, swarming around them with grinning faces, dragging their souls still hot and stinking from their bodies, down into the kingdom of death. I felt my temporal power with a joy greater than I had ever known, and so acute that I nearly lost consciousness. I felt how the world had, through me, been filled with terror and doom, and transformed from a brilliant feast to a place of fear and destruction. I brew my draught and princes and powerful nobles groan in their death pangs or wallow in their blood. I offer my potion and the guests at the lavish tables grow pale and their smiles fade and none raises his glass again or prates of love and the joy of living. For after my drink they forget all the beauty and wonder of life and a mist enfolds everything and their eyes fail and darkness falls. I turn down their torches and extinguish them so that it is dark. I assemble them with their unseeing eyes at my somber communion feast where they have drunk my poisoned blood, that which my heart drinks daily, but which for them spells death.

Il Toro sat motionless. His face was blue and his underjaw with its sparse beard viciously lowered as though he wanted to bite somebody with his brownish tusks. He was a frightful sight with his eyes bulging yellow and bloodshot from their sockets. Suddenly he twisted his hunched neck around as though trying to dislocate it, and the clumsy head lurched over on one side. At the same time his short bull body arched itself backward in a bow, jerked convulsively as though stabbed— and he was dead. By now all his men at the Prince's table were writhing in infernal agony, but it was not long before they too ceased to give any sign of life. As for Don Riccardo, he died leaning back with half-closed eyes as though reveling in my drink, much as he used to do when he had tasted a really rare wine; suddenly he threw out his arms as though wanting to embrace the whole world, fell backward, and died.

During the fighting and confusion nobody had any time for those who were dying, so they had to expire in their own way as best they could. Only Giovanni, who had been sitting on the same side as il Toro and who, thanks to the damned girl, had not tasted my potion, hurried forward to his father and stood bending over his horrible body as though under the delusion that he could help him. But a burly man with fists like those of a blacksmith elbowed his way to him just as the old scoundrel breathed his last, seized the lad as though he had been a feather and dragged him through the hall. The young coward allowed himself to be taken away and thus escaped us. Devil take him!

The tables were upset and their furnishings trampled underfoot by the combatants who were now quite insane with bloodlust. The women had fled shrieking, but in the midst of all the desolation I saw the Princess standing as though petrified, with rigid features and glassy eyes. Her cadaverous pallor contrasted comically with the paint which still remained on her middle-aged face. Some of the servants managed to lead her from that terrible room, and she followed them listlessly, as though unaware of where she was or whither they were conducting her.

Though inferior in number, il Toro's men still brandished their inadequate weapons as they retreated toward the exit doors. The battle continued on the stairs, and they were pursued down them and out into the square. Here the sorely pressed enemy was relieved by Montanza's bodyguard which had been summoned from the Palazzo Geraldi and, under cover of the latter, they contrived to make their escape from the town. Otherwise they would undoubtedly have been mowed down to the last man.

I stood there alone in the abandoned hall, now

in semidarkness since all the candelabra had been thrown onto the floor. Only the ragged, apparently half-starved urchins remained, creeping around with their torches and hunting among the corpses for scraps of food and grimy delicacies, which they devoured at incredible speed, simultaneously grabbing as much of the silver as they could hide beneath their tatters. When they judged it unsafe to stay any longer, they threw away their torches and stole out with their booty on padding naked feet, and I was left alone in the room. Undisturbed I gazed around me, sunk deep in thought.

The flickering rays of the dying torches illuminated the mutilated corpses of friend and foe, lying in their blood on the stone floor among the trampled bloodstained napery and the remnants of the great banquet. Their festal garments were torn and dirty and their pallid faces still twisted and evil, for they had died fighting in the midst of their mad fury. I stood there, surveying everything with my ancient eyes.

Brotherly love. Eternal peace.

How these creatures love to discuss themselves and their world in great and beautiful words!

When I waited on the Princess as usual the next morning in her bedchamber she was lying there supine with empty eyes and withered lips. Her mouth was closed as though it would never open again, and her hair was spread in a colorless tangle on the crumpled pillow. Her hands lay slack and motionless on the coverlet. She did not notice my presence though I was standing in the middle of the room watching her and waiting for her to express some behest. I could examine her as much as I wanted. The paint was still there but it was the only token of any kind of gaiety; her skin was dry and faded and her neck wrinkled despite its fullness. Her once expressive eyes stared blankly, all their radiance gone. It was incredible that she could ever have been beautiful, ever been loved and embraced by anybody. Even the thought of such a thing seemed grotesque. She was just an ugly woman lying there in bed. At last.

THE COURT is in mourning for its jester. The funeral took place today. All the household, the knights and nobles of the town followed him, and so of course did his own subordinates who must genuinely regret him, for it must be agreeable to be in the service of such a careless and extravagant master. Crowds stood gaping in the streets as the procession went on its way; the poor brutes are said to have liked the frivolous jackanapes. Oddly enough, such people appeal to them. While starving themselves, they enjoy hearing about the carefree extravagant lives of others. They are said to know all the stories about him, his escapades and successful "jests," and relate them in their dirty hovels around his palace. Now he was giving them an additional treat and letting them join in his magnificent funeral.

The Prince headed the cortege, with bowed grief-stricken head. He is always admirable when playing a part. Yet perhaps it is not really so admirable, since concealment is in his nature.

Nobody dared murmur a word. What they may subsequently say in their huts and palaces is of no importance. It has been represented as a fatal mistake; Don Riccardo chanced to drink the poisoned wine which was intended for the exalted guests. His unquenchable thirst being universally known, it is taken for granted that he was himself responsible for his tragic end. Apart from this everybody believes what he chooses. All are pleased that Montanza and his men should have been poisoned.

The Princess was not present at the funeral. She is still lying motionless and remote, refusing to eat. That is to say, she does not refuse, for she does not speak at all, but they cannot get anything down her throat. The stupid chambermaid bustles about, red-eyed and bewildered, sighing and mopping her pasty fat cheeks.

Nobody suspects me, for nobody knows who I am.

I⊤ MAY well be that he really mourns him; for such as he it is not impossible. I should imagine that he enjoys mourning him and finds it noble and 'seemly. Chivalrous selfless grief is always an elevating and agreeable sensation. Besides, he was very attached to him even if he did want him to die, and now that he has gone he cherishes him more than ever. Previously there was always something which hampered and disturbed his feelings for his friend, but now it exists no longer. Now that he has attained his desire he feels fonder than ever of him.

Everybody is talking about Don Riccardo, what he was like, how he lived and died, what he said and how splendidly he acted on this or that occasion, what a perfect knight he was, what a gay and gallant man. In a way he seems to be more alive than ever, but it is apt to be like that directly after a death. It soon passes over. Nothing is so sure as the final oblivion.

And yet they say that he will never be forgotten. And by falsifying him into something monstrously charming and extraordinary they hope to be able to keep him alive forever. They have a strange antipathy to death, especially in reference to some of their dead. His legend is in process of creation, and those who know the truth about this rake, this foolish empty-headed buffoon, must be amazed at the results. The fact that the whole thing is a lie from start to finish does not bother them in the least; to their minds he personified gaiety and poetry and God knows what, and now the world is no longer the same since they can never hear his horse-laughter again. His joyous pranks are ended, and they are altogether overwhelmed and distressed by their loss and the void he leaves behind him. They thoroughly enjoy mourning him.

The Prince joins most generously in this sentimental entertainment. He listens wistfully to the paeans of praise and sometimes adds a word of his own which seems all the more beautiful for having come from him. Otherwise I cannot help thinking that he is quite satisfied with his little assassin, his little bravo; though naturally he does not show it. He has not said a word to me on the subject, neither of praise nor blame. A prince need not pay any attention to his servants if he does not wish to.

He avoids me. He always does after that kind of thing.

The Princess makes no display of her grief. I do not quite know how this should be interpreted. Presumably it means that she mourns him deeply. But she just lies there staring.

I am the cause of her grief; and if she is desperate it is for my sake. If she is changed and never again will be as before, it is for my sake. If she lies there like an ugly old woman no longer caring about her appearance, that too is for my sake.

I could never have believed that I had such power over her.

THE MURDERS have made the Prince very popular. Everybody says that he is a great prince. Never before has he triumphed so over his enemies and been the object of such admiration. We are proud of him and consider that he has shown unusual cunning and energy.

Some wonder if any good can come out of it all. They say that they have evil premonitions, but somebody always has. The majority are delighted and cheer whenever he shows himself. Nearly everyone is susceptible to the charm of a prince who hesitates at nothing.

Now the people await a really peaceful and happy era. They think he did well to cut off the heads of the neighbors so that they can no longer disturb their happiness.

They think of nothing but their happiness.

I wonder what mighty schemes he is nursing now, if he meditates attacking them again, marching straight on their town and taking possession of it and the whole country. It would not be difficult, since all their leaders and chief citizens are out of the way. That child Giovanni is nothing to worry about, he will not cause us any trouble—a cowardly lad who runs away as soon as anything happens. He ought to be captured and taught how to behave like a man.

It is obvious that he means to harvest the fruits of the murders. Otherwise there would be no sense to it. He cannot content himself with things as they are. Of course one must reap that which one has sown.

There are some foolish rumors that Montanza's people have taken up arms in their anger and sworn to avenge their prince and his men. Of course that is only talk; it is quite likely though that they feel angry about it. They were meant to. But no one can believe that they should have taken up arms to avenge such a prince; even if they have it is of no consequence. A people without a leader is nothing but a miserable flock of sheep.

THEY SAY that an uncle of young Giovanni has taken command, and that it is he who has sworn revenge. That seems more credible. The people do not avenge their princes, why should they? Their life is the same under them all and they are thankful to be rid of at least one of their tormentors.

He is said to be a man of the same kidney as il Toro, but hitherto was never allowed to play an important part. His name is Ercole Montanza and he is reported to be dangerous, but no soldier. He seized the reins to save the country from the mortal peril which threatens it, according to himself, and at the same time he tries to set aside the youthful heir as being too weak for a prince, whereas he himself is of the true Montanza blood and therefore considers himself fitter to reign. This seems even more credible. It is just like most of the happenings in this world.

My prophecy may be on the way to fulfillment, that the youth with his hinds' eyes and the locket on his breast is destined never to sit on a throne.

CONSIDERABLE forces have been assembled to exact this vengeance and have already begun to pour into the country through the glen beside the river. Boccarossa leads them; together with his mercenaries he has undertaken to die for the new Montanza in exchange for a wage double that paid by our Prince. They burn and pillage and aim principally at helping others to die.

Our generals have hastily collected troops with which to check their advance. Once more the town is full of soldiers on their way to the front to resume their trade.

The Prince is doing nothing.

Our resources are limited, since so many men were killed in the former war. It is not easy to find sufficient men who can be used and know more or less what to do when under fire. However we are scraping together all that is left, and that ought to be as many as Montanza can collect, for they also have had grave losses which must have tapped their best blood. The enthusiasm is not quite the same as before, but our men submit themselves willingly, realizing that it is inevitable. They realize that they must accept their fate and that life is not meant for happiness alone.

The invaders are approaching the town and all checks are merely temporary. Our troops cannot resist them for long but must always end up by retreating. All the reports are depressing and monotonous, and mention only withdrawals and losses.

The enemy ravages the land through which he passes. The villages are plundered and burned and any inhabitants in his path are slain. The cattle are stolen, slaughtered, and roasted over the camp-fires, and what is over is taken in the baggage wagons for future use. The cornfields are burned. Now Boccarossa's legionaries can do as they please and they leave no living thing behind them.

Refugees trail into the town through the postern gate with their carts full of the queerest possessions, pots and pans, bedcovers and dirty rags, all kinds of old rubbish laughable in their worthlessness. Some of them lead a goat or a miserable cow by the horn, and they all look terrified. Nobody wants them here or knows why they have come. They sleep in the squares beside their beasts, and the town is beginning to look like a mucky village; the stink in their vicinity is appalling.

Our troops do nothing but withdraw. The enemy is said to be not so very far from the town, though I do not know exactly where, and the information is so shifting that one cannot keep track of it. Always the same wearisome reports that our men resisted but now are on the retreat, that now they are going to make a stand and then that they are obliged to retreat again. And the flood of refugees goes on just the same, filling the town with their cattle, their rags, and their jeremiads.

A queer war!

IN POINT of fact I quite understand the Prince's indifference and his readiness to leave everything to his staff. He is not interested in defensive tactics, they do not amuse him. He is like me—he likes to take the initiative. Ours is the spirit of attack. There is no pleasure in defending oneself, only an endless monotony with no glamour or excitement. And what is the use of it? It is too futile for words. Nobody can want to bother about anything like that. This is a boring war.

The Montanza - Boccarossa army can be seen from the city walls. This evening from my window up in the dwarfs' apartment I can see the light of their campfires on the plain. It is a fascinating sight in the darkness.

I can almost picture the faces of the mercenaries as they sit around the fires discussing the exploits of the day. They throw a few olive roots on the fire, and their features are hard and resolute in the light of its dancing flames. These are men who carry their fate in their hands and who do not live in perpetual suspense for the future. They light their campfires in any country and do not care which people provide their livelihood. It is all one to them which prince they serve—and in reality they serve only themselves. When they are weary they stretch themselves out in the darkness and rest for the morrow's slaughter. They are a people without a country, but the whole world is theirs.

It is a beautiful evening. The autumn air blows clear and cool from the mountains, and the stars must be shining. I have been sitting here for a long time at the window, watching the numerous fires. Now I too shall go to rest.

It is strange that I who can see the fires which are so far away cannot perceive the stars. I have never been able to. My eyes are not like others' but there is nothing the matter with them, for I can distinguish everything on earth very clearly.

I OFTEN think about Boccarossa. I can picture him, huge, nearly gigantic, with his pock-marked face, his animal jaw, and that gaze in the depths of his eyes. And the lion's mask on his breastplate, the grinning beast of prey sticking out its tongue at everything.

Our troops have come fleeing into the town after an engagement which was fought just outside the ramparts. It was a gory battle which cost us many hundred dead, not to mention the wounded who crawled in through the city gates or were dragged in by women who are said to have gone out to seek their sons and husbands on the battlefield.

Our soldiers were in a lamentable condition when they finally gave up and withdrew within the walls. Since their arrival there has been confusion in the town which is crammed to bursting, far too full of warriors, wounded and myriads of refugees from the countryside. Everything is one huge muddle, and the atmosphere is deplorable. People sleep in the streets though the nights are

beginning to be chilly, and even in the daytime
one can stumble over exhausted slumberers and
over the wounded whom nobody has any time to
attend to, though they may have had their hurts
bandaged. The whole thing is hopeless, and the
thought of the coming siege now that the enemy
has completely surrounded the city does not help
to disperse the utter despondency.

Is it worth while trying to resist somebody like
Boccarossa? Personally, I never anticipated any
success in this war.

But they say that the city is to be defended to
the last drop of blood, and also that it is strongly
fortified and can ho'd out for a long time, even
that it is impregnable. But so are all cities until
they are taken. I have my own opinion of its im-
pregnability.

The Prince has awakened and has begun to assume the leadership of the defense. He is unpopular and meets with no applause when he shows
himself. Folk think that the murder of Montanza
and his people was the act of a lunatic and can
lead to nothing but more war and misery.

The Princess is up and about again and has begun to eat a little, but she is not at all herself. She
has become much thinner and the skin of her erstwhile plump face is dry and gray. She really is
completely altered. Her clothes hang on her as

though they had been made for someone else. She goes dressed in black. When she speaks it is in a low almost whispering voice. Her mouth is still withered and her thinness has changed the expression of her face, the eye sockets are sunken and dark about the unnaturally burning eyes.

She kneels for hours in prayer before the crucifix, until her knees are so stiff and painful that she can scarcely rise. I have of course no idea what her prayers are about, but they cannot be answered since she goes on day after day.

She never leaves her room.

MAESTRO BERNARDO is said to be helping the Prince to strengthen the fortifications and inventing all kinds of ingenious arrangements for the defense of the town. Report says that the work is pursued with energy and goes on night and day.

I have great confidence in Maestro Bernardo's art and skill, but I do not think that he has much chance against Boccarossa. The old master is a great spirit, and his thoughts and knowledge comprehend nearly everything; indisputably he has great powers at his disposal which he has conquered from nature and which really obey him, presumably against their will. But Boccarossa seems to me as though he himself were one of those powers, as though they served him as a matter of course, and much more willingly. I think he is nearer nature.

Bernardo is a changed person, his haughty noble features always fill me with misgiving.

I think that it will be an unequal struggle.

If one saw them side by side, Bernardo with his philosopher's brow and Boccarossa with his powerful leonine jaw, there would be no doubt as to which were the stronger.

Food is beginning to run short in the town. Of course we do not notice it at the court, but they say the people are starving. Nor is that peculiar, with all the superfluous inhabitants who have no business to be here. The refugees are more and more disliked, being regarded, and rightly so, as the cause of the food shortage. They are a burden to the citizens. Most unpopular of all are their whining dirty children who go begging all over the place and are even said to steal when they get the chance. Bread is doled out twice a week but very little, for no preparations had been made for a siege and the stores are small. Soon they will come to an end. The refugees who had a cow or goat with them and lived on the milk have now slaughtered their emaciated beasts who were already nearly dead of starvation, and kept themselves alive with the meat which they could also exchange for flour and other necessities. Now they have nothing left and the townspeople affirm that they have hidden their meat and are better off than themselves, but I do not believe it, for they do not look like that. They are thin and seem very undernourished. This does not mean that I have any sympathy for these people; I share the town dwellers' aversion to them. They are stupid like all peasants, and spend most of their time sitting and staring. They have no intercourse with outsiders, but have divided themselves up according to their different villages and keep together in their dirty camps, the little bit of the square where they keep their old rags and which they seem to regard as a kind of home. In the evening they sit around their fires, if they have been able to procure any fuel, and talk in their imbecile language, of which scarcely a word is comprehensible. Nor would it be worth listening to if it were.

The filth and stench from all these people camping in the squares and streets is appalling. All this foulness is unbearable to me who am scrupulously clean about my person and very sensitive to any unpleasant features in my surroundings. Many consider that I am unduly susceptible in my detestation of human excrement and its smell. These primitive creatures are like the cattle with which they associate, and relieve themselves anywhere. It is too swinish for words. The air stinks of it and

I find the condition of the streets and squares so disgusting that I try to avoid going into the town. I do not have to carry so many messages now since the Princess' extraordinary change and Don Riccardo's timely death.

All these homeless people sleep in the open at night and cannot be too snug in their rags now that an unusually hard winter has set in. They say that some have been found frozen to death in the morning, that some scarecrow who remained prone when all the others had got up proved on closer examination to be dead. But they die more of their privations than of the actual cold, and then only the old folk who lack stamina and natural bodily warmth. Nobody minds their dying; they are only a burden to the others, and there are far too many people here in the town.

Boccarossa's men lack nothing. The whole country is at their disposal for plunder, and they make longer and longer forays into the interior to provide for their needs. They burn the villages as soon as they have taken what they want, and one can often see the reflection of distant fires in the sky at night. The surrounding district has long been completely devastated.

Oddly enough they have not yet attempted to storm the town. This surprises me, for it would have been an easy prey. Maybe they think that it is easier to starve it out; they have nothing against a siege when they can simultaneously pillage the countryside.

ANGELICA wanders listlessly about in idleness. Formerly she at least used to occupy herself with her embroidery. She is generally down by the river and sits there feeding the swans or merely watching it glide by. Sometimes she spends the whole evening at her window, gazing at the enemy's tents and bivouac fires and the plundered plain. I suppose that reminds her of her prince.

People look so strangely idiotic when they are in love, and particularly when they love in vain. The expression of their faces becomes peculiarly foolish and I cannot understand how anybody can say that love makes them more beautiful. Her eyes are, if possible, blanker and sillier than ever, and her cheeks are pale, not at all as they were during the banquet. But her mouth seems larger, the lips fuller, and it is plain that she is no longer a child.

Probably I am the only one who knows her criminal secret.

To my astonishment the Princess asked me today if I thought that Christ hated her. I answered quite truthfully that I knew nothing about it. She looked at me with her burning eyes and seemed distressed. But He must hate her, for He never allowed her any peace, and then He must hate her because of all her sins. I found this very likely and said so. The fact that I shared her opinion seemed to calm her and she sank into a chair, sighing deeply. I did not quite know what I was doing there, for as usual she had no task for me. After a moment I asked if I might go, and she replied that she had no power to decide that, but at the same time she gazed pleadingly at me as though she wanted me to help her. But I found the situation uncomfortable and went away. When I reached the doorway she flung herself on her knees before the crucifix and began desperately to gabble her prayers, clutching the rosary between her thin fingers.

It made a strange perplexing impression on me. What has happened to the old nincompoop?

OBVIOUSLY she genuinely believes that He hates her. She returned to the subject again today. She said that all her prayers were of no avail, for He still refused to forgive her. He will not listen to her and ignores her existence, except that He never allows her a moment's peace. It is so dreadful that she cannot endure it. I said that I thought she ought to appeal to her father confessor who has always shown such sympathy and understanding for her spiritual difficulties. She shook her head;

she had already done so, but he could give her no help. He did not understand her at all. He thought that she was without sin. I smiled sneeringly at this utterance from the smug monk.

Then she asked me what I thought of her. I said that I considered her a voluptuous woman and that I was sure that she was one of those who are destined to burn for all eternity in the fires of hell. At this, she flung herself on her knees before me and wrung her clasped hands so that the knuckles whitened, moaning and sighing and beseeching my mercy and deliverance in her great distress. I let her lie writhing at my feet, partly because I had no means of helping her and partly because I thought it was only right and proper that she should suffer. She seized my hand and moistened it with her tears, even tried to kiss it, but I pulled it back and would not let her carry on like that. This made her moan and whimper even more, and seemingly reduced her to a state of utter despair and agitation. "Confess thy sins!" I said, aware that my face was very stern. And she began to confess all her sins, her lewd life, her lawless affairs with men toward whom the devil had filled her with desire, and her voluptuous pleasure when she felt that she was ensnared in the devil's noose. I compelled her to describe her sins in detail and the horrible satisfactions they yielded and the names of those with whom she had had criminal rela-

tions. She obeyed all my commands and gave me a
terrible picture of her revolting life. But she did
not mention Don Riccardo and I commented on
this. She looked inquiringly at me and seemed not
to grasp my meaning. Was that too a sin? I in-
formed her that it was the most heinous of all. This
did not seem at all clear to her, and she looked at
me in wonder, almost in doubt. I could see that she
began to ponder what I had said, this notion which
was so foreign to her, and that her ponderings gave
her food for anxiety. I asked her whether she had
not loved him best of all. "Yes," she whispered, in
a scarcely audible voice, and fell to weeping again,
but not in the same way as before, more as most
people weep. She went on for so long that I had
no wish to stay there listening to her, but told her
that now I must go. She looked pleadingly and
hopelessly at me and asked if I could give her no
consolation. What could she do to make Christ
have mercy upon her? I answered that it was presumptuous of her to ask such a thing, for she was
so full of sin that it was natural that the Savior
should not listen to her prayers. He had not been
crucified for the redemption of such as she. She
listened meekly and said that she felt that too.
She was not worthly that He should listen to her.
She was aware of this in her innermost consciousness when she knelt praying before his image. She
sat down sighing, but somewhat calmer, and began

to talk about herself as the most depraved of all mankind, and that she never could share in the heavenly grace. "I have loved much," she said, "but I have not loved God and His Son, and so my punishment is only just."

Then she thanked me for my kindness. It was a relief to be able to confess, even if, as she well understood, she could not hope for any absolution. And it was the first time she had been able to weep.

I left her sitting there with red-rimmed eyes and her hair ruffled like an old birds' nest.

THE PRINCE spends much of his time with Fiammetta. Often they sit together alone after supper and I have to stay and wait upon them. At one time he used to linger there like that with the Princess, but very seldom. Fiammetta is quite a different type, cold, sedate, and unattainable, a real beauty. Her dark face is the hardest I have ever seen in a woman and if it were less lovely one would surely find it devoid of gentleness. There is an irresistible power about the coal-black eyes with their single spark.

I presume that she is frigid in love and not lavish with herself, but demands much and requires complete submission from those whom she con-descends to love. Perhaps the Prince likes this and is willing to put up with it. For all I know, coldness in love may be as much relished as warmth.

Personally I have nothing against her, unlike all the others. She treats the servants as though they were dust, and they say that they are not accustomed to such, that she is not their mistress but only a concubine. She does not seem to regard the other court ladies as her equals, but I wonder if she ever did, or if she ever has regarded anyone as her equal. It does not look like ordinary superciliousness, but more like an innate pride. Naturally they are furious, but they dare not show it, for if Madama should never return here, then Fiammetta might well replace her.

All the court says that she has let herself be "seduced" from sheer ambition, and that she is as cold-blooded as a fish, and that it is all extremely indecent. I do not understand what they mean, for, unlike the others who lower themselves to such infamies, she does not appear immodest.

Certainly the Prince is greatly charmed with her and is always exceedingly polite and witty in her presence. Otherwise he seems rather restless, nervous and irritable, and occasionally violent with his servants, and even with very distinguished persons. He was never like that before. They say that he is very annoyed over the development of events and not least over the people's discontent with him, for he is no longer what they call popular. He is particularly bad-humored when the hungry come and shout for bread beneath the castle windows.

I find it unworthy of a prince to pay any attention to the thoughts and sayings of the mob which surrounds him. They are always shouting for something. One would be kept very busy if one bothered with everything the people shout about.

They say that he has had the old court astrologer Nicodemus and the other long-beards secretly thrashed because of their extraordinarily favorable prophecies. It is not improbable. His father did so, though then it was because they prophesied something which opposed his wishes.

It is not easy to read the stars, and to read them so that men are pleased with what is written there.

In the town the situation is getting worse and worse; it is nothing less than sheer famine. Every day many die of hunger, or of cold and hunger combined, it is difficult to say which. The streets and squares are full of folk who cannot get up and who seem indifferent to their surroundings. Others wander about in an emaciated condition looking for something edible, or at least something with which to appease their hunger. Cats, dogs, and rats are hunted down and regarded as excellent fare. At the beginning of the siege the rats were held to be a menace to the refugee camps whose rubbish heaps attracted them, but now they are a desirable quarry. However, they are becoming more and more of a rarity. They seem to have had some kind of disease, for their corpses are all over the place, thereby failing the people when they were really needed.

I am not surprised that rats cannot endure living together with men like these.

Something incredible has happened. I shall try to relate it calmly and according to the sequence of events. This is not so easy, since I took a lively and important part in it all and have not yet got over the excitement. Now that it is well and I may say successfully over, giving me every reason to feel satisfied with the result and my own share in it, I shall dedicate part of the night to the chronicling of it.

Late last night I was sitting at my window in the dwarfs' apartment and looking out over Boccarossa's campfires as I frequently do before retiring, when I suddenly saw a figure creeping furtively through the trees down by the river, toward the eastern wing of the palace. I thought it strange that anybody should be down there at such an hour and wondered if it could be a member of the household. The moon was shining, but so hazily that I could scarcely distinguish the figure. He seemed to be wrapped in a wide cloak and hastened toward the wing where he disappeared through one of the lesser doors. Presumably, he must belong to the palace, since he knew it so well. But something in his deportment roused my suspicions as did his behavior in general, so I decided to clear up the mystery and hurried out into the night, re-entering through the same door as he. It was pitch dark on the stairs, but I know them better than any other because of the many times I was obliged to mount them in the old days. They lead to Angelica's room among others; and now to hers alone, since none of the other apartments are in use.

I felt my way up to her door and listened outside it. My suspicions had paved the way for such a possibility, yet I was amazed to hear two voices within. One of them was Giovanni's!

They spoke in whispers, but my keen ears heard everything. I was the invisible witness of a touching and unbounded "happiness." "Beloved!" panted one of them, and the other whispered in answer: "Beloved! Beloved!" again and again—nothing else, and their conversation was far from interesting from an outsider's point of view. If it had not been so terribly serious I should have found this monotonous repetition of the same word perfectly ridiculous, but unfortunately there was nothing ridiculous about it. I felt my entire body chill to ice as I heard their tender and unsuspecting use of the word, though they would have been petrified with horror if they had given a thought to its inner meaning and its significance on *their* lips. Then I heard the two criminals kissing each other, several times, simultaneously assuring each other of their love in a most childish stammering manner. It was gruesome.

I hurried away. Where could I find the Prince? Was he still at the supper table in the dining room where I had left him with Fiammetta scarcely an hour ago? As usual I had waited upon them until told that he had no further need of my services.

No further need of my services! The expression seemed strange as I felt my way hastily down the stairs in the darkness. One always needs the services of one's dwarf.

I ran over the courtyard to the archway which connects the old and new wings. Here too the stairs and corridors were pitch dark, but I continued on my way and, at last, stood breathless outside the great double doors. I listened. Nothing. But they might still be there. I should have liked to make sure, but to my annoyance I could not open the door, for it was one of those which are too high for me to manipulate. I listened again and then had to go away without being quite certain.

I continued to the Prince's bedchamber. It is not so far away, but on the floor above. I approached his door and listened again, but there too it was silent. I could hear nothing indicative of his presence in the room. Perhaps he was already sleeping? It was not impossible. Dare I wake him? No, it was out of the question, I could never dream of doing such a thing. But my errand was of such tremendous importance. Never before had I had such an urgent one.

I plucked up my courage and knocked. There was no answer. I knocked again, as hard as I could with my clenched fist. No reply.

He could not be there, for I know what a light sleeper he is. Where was he? I became more and more nervous. All this took so *long!* Where could he be?

Maybe he was with Fiammetta? They might have withdrawn there so as to be absolutely undisturbed. It was my last hope.

I rushed down the stairs again and into the courtyard. Fiammetta lives in another part of the palace, presumably to disguise her relationship with the Prince. One must cross the courtyard to get there.

I came in through the right arch, but not being so familiar with that part of the castle I had difficulty in finding my way; I mounted the wrong staircase and had to descend and start all over again, and then I had great trouble in keeping my bearings through all the dark corridors. I kept getting more and more irritated at the thought of all the time I was losing and I hurried up and down them without finding what I was looking for. I felt like a mole wandering about in his burrow hunting for something. Luckily I can see in the dark like a mole; my eyes seem to be made for that. I knew the position of her window on the castle wall and eventually I managed to find the right direction and arrived at her door.

I listened. Was there anyone inside? Yes.

The first thing I heard was Fiammetta's cool laugh. I had never heard her laugh before, but I knew at once that it must be hers. It was rather hard and perhaps a trifle artificial, yet tantalizing in its way. Then I heard the Prince laugh, briefly and subduedly. I began to breathe again.

After that I heard their voices fairly well, though not what they said, for they must have been far inside the room. But they were indulging in a real conversation and not merely repeating the same word to each other. I do not know if they were talking about love, but I doubt it. I didn't think it sounded like that. Then there was a sudden silence, and, though I strained by ears to the uttermost, I could hear nothing. But after a while I caught an unpleasant snorting sound and realized that they were doing something disgusting. I felt a slight nausea. I did not believe that my state of excitement would permit me to be physically sick, but nevertheless I went down the corridor, as far as I dared without risking missing the Prince, and stood waiting there. I waited as long as possible so as to avoid hearing that nasty sound again. I felt as though I had been standing there for an eternity.

When at last I returned to the door they were lying and chatting about something, I know not what. The unexpected change astonished as much as it pleased me, and I hoped soon to be able to fulfill my mission. However, they did not hurry themselves, but remained lying there talking no doubt about matters of no importance whatsoever. It irritated me beyond words to hear them and think of all the invaluable time that was being lost. But I was helpless. I dared not make my presence known and surprise them in such a situation.

At last I heard the Prince get up, still discussing something with her on which they were not of the same mind, and begin to dress himself. I went far away from the door and stood on watch in the darkness.

When he came out he went straight toward me without knowing it. "Your Grace," I whispered, keeping at a cautious distance from him. He was furious when he realized my presence and burst out into the most opprobrious epithets and threats. "What are you doing here? What are you spying on? Foul little monster! Slimy snake! Where are you? Let me crush you!" And he fumbled after me in the corridor with outstretched hands, but could not catch me in the dark. "Let me speak! Let me tell you what it is all about!" I said coldly, though in reality I was beside myself. At last he let me do so.

Now I told him straight out that his daughter was in process of being raped by Lodovico Montanza's son who had crept into the castle to avenge his father and bring eternal shame and dishonor to her and all his house. "It's a lie!" he shrieked. "What crazy invention is this? It's a lie!" "No, it is the truth," I cried, and stepped fearlessly forward. "He is in her chamber and my own ears have witnessed the preparations for the crime. Now you are too late, the deed has already been done, but maybe you will still find him with her." I saw that now he believed me, for he was as though thunderstruck. "Impossible!" he said, but at the same time he began to hurry toward the gate. "Impossible!" he repeated. "How could he get into the city? And the palace—it is guarded!" Running at full speed to keep pace with him, I replied that I did not understand that either, but I had first seen him down by the river, and he might have come over it on a raft or something similar—

who knows what such a foolhardy lad can think of —and from there straight into the courtyard. "Impossible!" he maintained. "Nobody can come into the town over the river, between the fortresses on both banks with their culverins where archers keep watch night and day. It is absolutely unthinkable!" "Yes, it is unthinkable," I admitted. "It is impossible to grasp and the devil knows how he was able to get here, but here he is all the same. I am quite certain that it was his voice I heard."

We had reached the courtyard. The Prince hastened toward the postern to give orders to the watch to keep strictest reinforced guard over the whole castle, so that he should have no chance of escape. His precautions were wise and reasonable —but think if the criminal had already slipped away! Or if both had fled! The horrible suspicion sent me flying over the courtyard as fast as my legs could carry me, and up the stairs to Angelica's door.

I put my ear against it. No sound within! *Had they fled?* My own heart was beating so violently after my wild dash and with agitation at the thought of their possible escape, that it might prevent me from hearing any other sound. I tried to calm myself, to breathe gently and regularly—and listened again. No, there was no sound at all from the room. I raged, I thought I should go mad! At last I could bear the suspense no longer; gently, without so much as a click, I succeeded in opening the door. Through the crack I could see that there was a light within—but not a sound, nothing to show that there was anybody there. I slipped inside and immediately recovered my composure. To my joy I saw them sleeping side by side in her bed, by the light of a little oil lamp that they had forgotten to extinguish. They had fallen asleep like a pair of exhausted children after making their first acquaintance with the bestial instincts of love.

I took the lamp, went forward and let its light shine on them. They lay with their faces turned toward each other, their mouths half open, blushing and still excited by the terrible crime which they had committed, and of which, sleeping, they seemed no longer aware. Their eyelashes were moist, and small drops of sweat beaded their upper lips. I regarded their slumber, almost innocent in its foolish thoughtlessness and its oblivion of all danger and the outside world. Is this what human beings call happiness?

Giovanni lay on the outer edge of the bed, with a lock of black hair across his forehead and a faint smile on his lips as though he had performed a noble and successful feat. Around his neck hung the narrow gold chain with the medallion containing the portrait of his mother, who is supposed to be in paradise.

Now I heard the Prince and his men on the stairs, and presently he came in followed by two sentinels, one of whom carried a torch. The room was lighted up, but nothing disturbed the pair in their deep slumber. He almost stumbled as he went forward to the bed and saw his incomparable shame. Livid with wrath he snatched the sword from one of the sentinels and with a single blow severed Giovanni's head from his body. Angelica woke up and stared with wild dilated eyes as they dragged her gory lover from her couch and flung him on to the muckheap outside the window. Then she fell back in a swoon and did not recover consciousness as long as we remained in the room.

The Prince shook with agitation after this well-wrought deed and I saw how he supported himself with one hand on the doorpost as he went out of the room. I too quitted it and went back to my own apartment. I went slowly, for there was no further need for haste. In the courtyard I saw the torch guiding the Prince on his way; it disappeared beneath the archway as though it had been extinguished in the dark.

ANGELICA is still unconscious; she is sick of a fever which the court physician does not understand. Nobody sympathizes with her. It is taken for granted that she made no real resistance when she was seduced, and therefore her rape is regarded as an unsurpassed disgrace for the princely house and the whole realm. She is being tended by an old woman. Nobody from the court visits her.

The body of her infamous lover has been thrown into the river, since it was not desirable that it should remain lying outside the palace. I hear that it was not submerged by the whirlpools but was borne out to sea by the current.

A rather odd disease has made its appearance in the town. The first symptoms are said to be ague and a terrible headache, then the eyes and tongue swell so that speech is impossible, and the whole body reddens and impure blood transpires through the skin. The sick cry out constantly for water, because they have a fire burning within them. The doctors are helpless—but when are they anything else? Nearly all the infected are said to have died, but I do not know how many that may be.

Naturally there are no cases here at the court. It is confined to the poorest and hungriest, principally the refugees, and is doubtless due to the incredible filth in their camps and everywhere in the town. I am not surprised that they should die of all the ordure that surrounds them.

Angelica cannot be sick of this plague. Her malady is the same as that which she once had as a child. I do not quite remember when, nor the exact circumstances. She has always been rather sickly, for reasons which could not possibly affect anybody else's health. Ah, now I remember. It was when I cut off her kitten's head.

THE PLAGUE is spreading more and more, from day to day. Now not only the poor, but anybody can catch it. The houses are full of moans and so are the streets and squares, for at least as many are living there. Passers-by can see the sick tossing on their ragged beds on the paving stones and giving vent to loud despairing shrieks. The pains are said to be uncommonly severe and drive some of the sufferers nearly insane. A tour around the town is apparently quite revolting, and the descriptions are full of repulsive and almost unbearable details. The breath of the smitten is like an appalling miasma and the body is covered with foul boils which burst and discharge their disgusting contents. I cannot hear these accounts without feeling physically sick.

Few hesitate to blame the refugees for this fearful plague, and they are hated worse than ever. But some maintain that it is really a divine punishment for the sins of mankind. They say the people suffer this in order that the Lord may cleanse them of their wickedness, and that they must submit patiently to His will.

I am quite prepared to regard it as a punishment, but whether it is their God who wields the scourge—that I know not. It may just as well be another and darker power.

THE PRINCESS leads a strange life. She never leaves her room which is always in semi-darkness because the windows are veiled with thick draperies. She says that she is not worthy to rejoice in the sunlight and that it is not right to do so. The walls are bare, and there are no chairs or tables, only a prie-dieu and above it a crucifix. It looks like a nun's cell. While the bed is still there, she does not lie in it, but on a heap of straw on the floor which is never changed and which becomes more and more musty and odoriferous. It is stifling in there and I can scarcely breathe the stuffy air. On first entering, it is impossible to distinguish anything until one becomes accustomed to the half light. Then one perceives her, half dressed, with rumpled hair, utterly indifferent to her appearance. Her eyes are febrile and her cheeks thin and sunken, for she mortifies her flesh and eats practically nothing. That stupid peasant lass of a tire-woman goes about complaining because she cannot persuade her mistress to eat. Sometimes the Princess nibbles a morsel to make the silly wench stop crying. The girl herself is plump and chubby cheeked and devours everything she can get hold of. Howling and whimpering, she wolfs the tempting dishes which her mistress waves aside.

The penitent spends most of her time in front of the crucifix, kneeling and repeating her fruitless prayers. She knows that they are of no avail and, before beginning, she puts up a special prayer to the Crucified One that he may forgive her for turning once more to Him. Sometimes she lays aside her rosary in despair and, fixing her burning eyes on her Savior, improvises her own prayers. But still He does not hear her and on arising she is as unredeemed as when she first started. Often she has not the strength to rise without the assistance of her maid. She has even been known to collapse from sheer exhaustion and remain prone on the floor until the girl found her there and had her dragged onto the straw.

She believes that she is the cause of all our misfortunes and that all the suffering and the horrors are due to her sinfulness. I do not know how much she realizes of what is going around her; one would think that she had only the vaguest idea of it all. Yet she must have a faint notion that it is full of horror. All the same, I believe that she is really indifferent to this world and all that happens here and considers it of no importance. She lives in a private world with her own problems and troubles.

Now she knows that her greatest sin was her love for Don Riccardo. Because of it, she clung to this life and treasured it. She says that she loved him above everything, that her feelings for him filled her whole being and made her very happy. One should not love a human being as much as that. Only God may be loved like that.

I do not know how much her degradation is due to my revelation of her criminal life and the hellfire which awaits her. I have described the pains of the damned and she has listened meekly to my expositions. Of late she has begun to scourge herself.

She is always very grateful when I come to her. I avoid visiting her too often.

ANGELICA has recovered from her sickness and is up and about again, but she never appears at meals or at the court. I have seen her now and again in the rose garden or sitting down by the river, staring at it. Her eyes are, if possible, larger than ever and quite glassy. They look as though she saw nothing with them.

I noticed that she was wearing Giovanni's locket around her neck and that it was stained with blood. Presumably she found it in the bed and cherishes it as a souvenir of him. But she might have begun by washing off the blood.

Now that I think of it, the mother is in paradise while her son languishes in hell-fire, having died without prayer or sacrament while sleeping the deep slumber of sin. So they can never meet. Perhaps Angelica prays for his soul. Her prayers are sure to be in vain.

No one knows what she is thinking about. She has not uttered a word since she woke up that night or, rather, since her last word to her lover. With my knowledge of their conversation I can almost guess what that word was.

THOSE WHO consider the plague and all the rest a punishment from God which should not be eluded but gratefully accepted with thanks to the Almighty, now go about the streets proclaiming their beliefs and scourging themselves in order to help the Lord redeem their souls. They go in groups, hollow-eyed and so emaciated that they could not remain erect were they not in ecstacy. People follow them everywhere, and their behavior is said to be causing a religious revival. Home, family, occupation, even dying relations, are abandoned and the survivors join the penitents. Every once in a while somebody gives vent to a crazy triumphant scream, pushes his way into the group and begins to scourge himself, to the accompaniment of shrill desperate cries. Then everybody begins to praise the Lord and the folk in the street fall on their knees. Earthly life and its familiar horrors, of which they have seen too much, have no more interest nor value for them. They think only of their souls.

The priests are said to look askance at these fanatics because they tempt people away from the churches and their own solemn processions which are replete with holy images and choir boys swinging perfumed censers in the stinking streets. They say these self tormentors lack faith, and evade the consolations of religion, thanks to their gross exaggerations. God cannot regard this with approval or pleasure. But I think if anyone is truly religious, it is those who are so much in earnest about their faith. The priests do not seem to like it if their teachings are taken too seriously.

But there are many others on whom the horrors have had another effect, who now love life better than ever before and cling to it madly in their fear of death. The revelry goes on night and day in some of the city's palaces, and one hears of the wildest orgies taking place within their walls. Many of the poorest and meanest are affected in the same way and, as far as they are able, do likewise, wallowing in the sole vice at their command. They cling to their miserable lives and do anything not to lose them. When the small portions of bread are doled out here at the postern gate, the poor wretches can be seen fighting for the scraps, ready, if need be, to tear each other to pieces.

But there are said to be others who sacrifice themselves for their fellows. They nurse the sick though there is no point in that, since they merely expose themselves to infection. They disregard death and the rest, and so do not seem to realize the risks they are running. They are akin to the religious maniacs though they express themselves differently.

If one is to believe the tales which have come to my ear, the people down in the town continue to live just as before, each according to his kind and nature. The only difference is a more exaggerated and hysterical manner, and the net result is quite valueless from God's point of view. Therefore, I wonder if it really was He who sent them the plague and the other trials.

Today Fiammetta passed me. Naturally, she did not deign to look at me. But how flawlessly beautiful she is in her aloofness! She is like a gentle zephyr among the foulness and agitation which surround her. There is a coolness about her person and her proud inaccessible nature which inspires peace and security. She does not let herself be influenced by the horrors of life, instead she rules over them; she can even make use of them. Imperceptibly, with dignity, and almost as a matter of course, she is beginning to assume the Princess' place as the mistress of the court. The others realize that there is nothing to be done about it and adapt themselves accordingly. One cannot help admiring her.

Had it been anybody else who passed without deigning to throw me a glance, I should have been furious. With her it seemed quite natural.

I can quite understand why the Prince loves her. Not that I ever could myself, but that is quite different. Could I ever really love anybody? I do not know. If I could love, it would have been the Princess. But now I hate her instead.

And yet I do feel that she is the only one whom I could ever have loved. Why that should be is quite beyond me. I do not understand it at all.

Truly love is something of which one knows nothing.

ANGELICA has drowned herself in the river.

She must have done it yesterday evening or last night, for nobody saw her. She left a letter behind which leaves no doubt that she killed herself in that manner. Throughout the day they have been searching for her body, all the length of the river where it flows through the beleaguered city, but in vain. Like Giovanni's, it must have been carried away by the ripples.

There is a great to-do at the court. Everybody is upset and cannot realize that she is dead. I find it very understandable: her beloved is dead, and now so is she. They all moan and weep and reproach themselves but, above all, they discuss the letter, relating its contents to each other and reading it again and again. The Prince was apparently very distressed when he heard of it, and, on the whole, seems upset by it. The damigellas sob and sigh and melt into tears over the touching phrases in the letter. I cannot understand their behavior. I see nothing extraordinary about the letter, and it changes nothing—certainly not the crime which was committed and which everybody condemned unanimously. It contains nothing new.

I had to hear it again and again until I know it almost by heart. It runs something like this:

I do not want to stay with you any longer. You have been so kind to me, but I do not understand you. I do not understand how you could take my beloved away from me, my dear one who came so far from another country to tell me that there was a thing called love.

I did not know that such a thing existed, but as soon as I saw Giovanni I knew that love was the only reality in the world and that everything else was nothing. As soon as I met him, I knew why life had been so strangely difficult up to then.

Now I do not want to stay here, where he is not,

but I shall follow him. I have prayed to God and He has promised to let me meet Giovanni and we shall always be together. But He would not say where He was going to take me. I shall just lay myself down to rest on the river, and He will take me where I am to go.

You must not believe that I have taken my life, for I have only done as I was told. And I am not dead. I have gone to be joined forever to my be- loved.

I am taking the medallion with me even though it does not belong to me. I have been told to do so. I have opened it and the portrait inside has filled me with an endless longing to leave this world.

She has asked me to say that she forgives you. I, too, forgive you with all my heart.

Angelica.

The Princess is convinced that she is the cause of Angelica's death. This is the first time I have ever known her to take any interest in her child. She scourges herself more than ever to efface this sin, eats nothing at all, and prays to the Crucified One for forgiveness.

The Crucified One does not answer.

THIS MORNING the Prince sent me with a letter to Maestro Bernardo in Santa Croce. It is a long time since he was seen at court and of late I have almost forgotten his existence.

Much against my will, I went out into the town, for I have not been there since the plague began to rage. Not that I fear the disease. But certain things have a disagreeable effect on me, I am almost afraid of having to see them. My reluctance was quite justified, for the sights which I was compelled to witness were really quite appalling. At the same time it was a remarkable experience which filled me with a kind of somber savagery and an awareness of the vanity and ruin of everything. My path was lined with the sick and dying. Those who were already dead were being collected by the funeral Brothers in their black hoods with the terrifying eyeholes. They appeared everywhere, giving a spectral touch to the scene. I felt as though I were wandering in the kingdom of the dead. Even the untainted were branded by death. They crept about the streets hollow-eyed and emaciated, like phantoms from the time when the world was still alive. It was gruesome to see the somnambulistic accuracy with which they avoided treading on the bundles which lay everywhere in their path and which might be either dead or alive. One could not really see. It is impossible to conceive anything more lamentable than these victims of the plague, and I was obliged frequently to turn aside to prevent myself from vomiting. Some were clad in the poorest rags through which one could see the most loathsome boils on the bluish-tinted skin which indicated that the end was near. Others screamed madly to show that their bodies still lived, while others lay unconscious, their uncontrolled limbs twitching unceasingly. Never before have I seen such a spectacle of human degradation. The eyes of some shone with the bottomless glint of madness and they rushed forward, despite their weakness, toward those who had fetched water from the wells for the sick, snatching so violently at the ladle that nearly all the water was spilled on the ground. Others crawled along the street like animals to reach the much longed-for wells which seemed to be the goal for all these wretches.

They were creatures who had ceased to behave like human beings and had lost every sentiment of human dignity in an effort to cling to their utterly worthless lives. I cannot even talk of the stink of all this misery; the mere thought of it makes me retch. There were bonfires in the squares where stacks of corpses were being burned, and their pungent odor was felt everywhere. A thin smoke hung over the whole town and, all the while, the churchbells tolled their never ceasing knell.

As so often before, I found Maestro Bernardo deep in contemplation before his Holy Communion. He sat with his grizzled head somewhat bowed and he looked much older. His Christ sat at the supper table, breaking bread and handing it to all who were gathered there; His hair and brow were haloed by the same celestial light as before. The wine chalice was being passed around the table which was covered by a pure white cloth. There were no hungry or thirsty there. But the old man seemed pensive and heavy-hearted among his paintbrushes.

He did not reply when I said that I had a letter for him from the Prince, but gestured to show that I could put it down somewhere. He would not let himself be snatched from his world. What kind of world?

I left Santa Croce full of thought.

On my way home I passed the campanile, the one that is going to be loftier than any other. Work has, of course, been stopped on it during the war and it has been quite forgotten. There it stands half finished and the top layer of stones is uneven because the building was stopped in the middle. It is like a ruin. But the bronze reliefs at the base representing scenes from the life of the Crucified One are quite finished and very successful.

It has all turned out exactly as I said.

THE WHOLE palace is decked in black. The walls and furniture are covered with black cloth and the inmates tread softly and speak in whispers.

The damigellas have black satin gowns and the courtiers black velvet suits and black gloves.

Angelica's death has given rise to all this; her life gave rise to nothing at all. But the people here literally enjoy mourning. Their grief for Don Riccardo has been succeeded by the mourning for her, and so at last he is really dead. But now they do not discuss the deceased, for there is nothing to discuss. She was so utterly devoid of interest. Besides, nobody knew what she was really like. They merely mourn for her. Everywhere one hears sighs not only over the young Princess' fate, but even over the fate of Giovanni, he who belonged to the enemy, the most hated of all the princely families; sighs over their love, of which there is no longer the slightest doubt, and over their death for the sake of their love. Death and love being their pet subjects, they think it is delightful to weep over them, especially when the two happen to be united into one.

The Prince seems rather overcome. I imagine that is why he is so reserved and uncommunicative. At least he is so with me, and yet I have sometimes had the pleasure of receiving his confidences, but that was on very different occasions. Now it seems as though he avoids me, I do not think he makes use of me quite as often as before. For instance, he did not personally give me the letter to Bernardo, but sent it by one of the courtiers.

Sometimes I think that he is almost beginning to fear me.

That red-cheeked peasant wench of the Princess' is sick. At last she has lost some of her rubicundity. I wonder what can be the matter with her?

It is odd, but I do not fear the plague at all. I have a feeling that I shall never catch it, that it cannot affect me. Why? I just feel like that about it.

It is for human beings, for these creatures around me. Not for me.

The Princess sinks lower and lower. It is almost painful to witness her decline, the dissolution taking place within her, the neglect, indifference, and dirt which surround her. The sole trace of her birth and former personality lies in the obstinacy and fortitude with which she fulfills her destiny and prevents those around her from exercising any influence upon it.

Since the chamberwoman's sickness, nobody is allowed to come near her and the room is in a worse state than ever. Now she eats nothing at all and is so emaciated that I can scarcely understand how she keeps alive.

I am her only visitor. She begs me to come and help her in her great need, to let her confess her sins to me.

I AM rather agitated. I have come straight from her and am terrifyingly conscious of the power which I sometimes exercise over human beings. I shall describe this visit.

As usual, I could see nothing at first. Then the windows outlined themselves, despite their thick curtains, as lighter parts of the wall, and I saw her crouching there by the crucifix, busy with her eternal praying. She was so absorbed in her orisons that she did not hear me open the door.

The room was so stifling that I could scarcely breathe. It was revolting. Everything nauseated me: the smell, the half-light, her shrunken body, the thin indecently exposed shoulders, the sinews ridging her neck, the untidy hair like an old birds' nest, all that once had been worthy of love. A kind of fury convulsed me. I may hate human beings, but I do not like to see their degradation.

Suddenly I heard myself shouting furiously in the darkness, before she had noticed me or become aware of my presence.

"Why are you praying? Have I not told you that you may not pray? That I do not want your prayers?"

She turned around, not in fear but moaning softly like a flogged bitch with her eyes fixed humbly on me. That kind of thing does nothing to mitigate a man's anger.

I went on mercilessly: "Do you think He cares about your prayers, that He forgives you because you kneel there, begging and praying and perpetually confessing your sins? It is easy enough to confess sins. Do you think He lets himself be fooled by that? Do you think He doesn't see through you?

"It is Don Riccardo whom you love, not Him! Do you think I don't know that? Do you think you can cheat me, deceive me with your devilish arts, with your penances, your scourgings of your lascivious body? You are longing for your lover though you say that you long for the One on the wall there! It is he whom you love!"

She looked at me in terror and her bloodless lips trembled. Then she flung herself at my feet groaning: "It is true! It is true! Save me! Save me!"

Her confession moved me powerfully.

"Voluptuous whore!" I exclaimed. "Feigning love for your Savior while in secret you lie with a lecher from hell! Betraying your God with one whom He has cast into the depths of hell! Diabolical woman, fixing your eyes on the Crucified One and proclaiming your burning love for Him, while all your soul rejoices in the embraces of another! Don't you realize that He hates you? Don't you realize it?"

"Yes, yes," she moaned and writhed like a trodden worm at my feet. It revolted me to see her cringing like that, it irritated me and oddly enough her behavior gave me no pleasure. She stretched out her hands to me. "Punish me, punish me, thou scourge of God!" she whimpered. She groped for the scourge on the floor and handed it to me and huddled up like a dog in front of me. I seized it, half-furious and half-nauseated, it whistled through the air over her loathsome body, and all the time I heard myself shrieking: "It is the Crucified One! He who hangs on the wall is scourging you now, He whom you have kissed so often with your glowing lying lips, whom you have professed to love! Do you know what love is? Do you know what He requires of you?

"I have suffered for you, but you have never cared about that! Now you shall know what it feels like to suffer!"

I was beside myself, I scarcely knew what I was doing. Knew? Of course I knew! I was taking revenge, retribution for everything! I was dispensing justice! I was exercising my terrible power over mankind! Yet I took no real pleasure in it.

She made no complaint while it was going on. On the contrary, she was very quiet and still, and when it was over she lay there as though I had relieved her of her sorrow and unrest.

"Burn forever in the fires of the damned! May

the flames eternally lick the foul belly which has rejoiced in the horrible sin of love!"

With this judgment I left her, lying there on the floor as though in a swoon.

I went home. With thudding heart I mounted the stairs to the dwarfs' apartment and shut the door behind me.

While writing this, my agitation has subsided, and I experience nothing but an endless void and boredom. My heart thuds no longer, I cannot feel it at all. I stare in front of me and my lonely countenance is dark and joyless.

Maybe she was right when she said that I was a scourge of God.

It is the evening of the same day and I am sitting here looking out over the town below. It is twilight and the bells have ceased their tolling and the domes and houses are beginning to fade away. In the half-light I can see the smoke from the funeral pyres coiling between them and the pungent smell reaches up to my nostrils. A thick veil shrouds everything, soon it will be quite dark.

Life! What is the point of it? What is its meaning, its use? Why does it go on, so gloomy and so absolutely empty?

I turn its torch downward and extinguish it against the dark earth, and it is night.

The peasant girl is dead. Her red cheeks could not stop her from dying. The plague took her, though for a long time nobody would believe it because she did not suffer the same pains as the others.

Fiammetta is dead too. She sickened this morning and after a couple of hours she was gone. I saw her when the phantoms from the Brotherhood came to fetch her. She was a horrible sight: her face was swollen and misshapen and presumably her body likewise. She was no longer a thing of beauty, but merely a disgusting corpse. They laid a cloth over her monstrous features and went away.

Here at the court they are terrified of the plague and want to get the dead out of the way as quickly as possible. But the order has been given that she is to be buried tonight with special honors. It does not really matter much, since she is dead.

Nobody mourns her.

Perhaps the Prince mourns her, in fact he surely does. Or perhaps he feels slightly relieved. Perhaps both.

Nobody knows, for he speaks to no one. He goes about pale and worn and is no longer himself. His forehead is furrowed beneath the black fringe and he is a little bent. His dark eyes gleam strangely and are full of unrest.

I caught a glimpse of him today and it was then I noticed it. I have seen him very seldom of late. I do not serve at his table.

I have not visited the Princess since that last time. I hear she is in a coma. Now that Fiammetta is dead, they say the Prince visits her frequently, sitting by her bed and watching over her.

Human beings are so strange, I can never understand their love for each other.

THE ENEMY raised the siege and went away as soon as the plague began to spread among them. Boccarossa's mercenaries have no desire to fight such a foe.

And so, the plague has put an end to the war as nothing else could have done. Both countries are pillaged, particularly our own. The populations are probably too exhausted after two wars to be able to go on. Montanza has achieved nothing and maybe his troops will take the pest home with them.

More and more people are dying here in the palace. The black hangings in honor of Angelica are still up and match the somber atmosphere.

I am quite excluded from the service of the court. Nobody summons me any longer, nobody has any orders for me. Least of all the Prince; I never set eyes on him at all.

I can see on everybody's faces that there is something in the wind, but I do not know what it can be.

Has somebody maligned me?

I have withdrawn altogether to the dwarfs' apartment where I live quite alone. I do not even go down to eat, but keep myself alive on a little old bread which I have up here. It is quite sufficient, I have never wanted much.

I sit here alone under the low ceiling, deep in thought.

I like this utter solitude more and more.

It is a long time since last I wrote anything in this book of mine. That is because things have happened which strongly affected my life and made it impossible for me to continue with my notes. I could not even get hold of them, and only now have I had them brought to me here.

I am sitting chained to the wall in one of the castle dungeons. Until recently, my hands were also manacled, though that was quite superfluous. I could not possibly escape. But it was meant to aggravate my punishment. Now at last I have been freed from them. I do not know why. I have not asked for it, I have asked for nothing. Thus it is a little more bearable now, though my condition has not changed. I have persuaded Anselmo my jailer to fetch my writing materials and notes from the dwarfs' apartment so that I may have some slight recreation by occupying myself with them. He may have risked something by getting them for me, for though my hands have been freed it is not at all certain that they do not grudge me this little pastime. As he said, he has no right to grant me anything, however much he may wish it. But he is an obliging and very simple fellow, so at last I managed to persuade him to do it.

I have read through my notes from the beginning, a little every day. It has been a certain satisfaction thus to relive my own and several others' lives and once again meditate over everything in the silent hours. I shall now try to continue from where I left off and thus provide myself with a little variety in my somewhat monotonous existence.

I do not really know how long I have been here. My time in prison has been so utterly uneventful, each day precisely like all the others, that I have stopped reckoning them and take no further interest in the passage of time. But I clearly recall the circumstances which led me to this dungeon and chained me to its wall.

One morning I was sitting peacefully in my dwarfs' chamber when one of the assistant torturers

suddenly came in through the door and commanded me to follow him. He gave no explanation and
I asked him no questions, considering that it was
beneath my dignity to address him. He took me
down to the torture chamber where stood the executioner, big and ruddy and stripped to the waist.
There was a lawyer there too, and after I had been
shown the instruments of torture he exhorted me
to make a full confession of all that had happened
during my visits to the Princess, which, they said,
had been the cause of her present deplorable condition. Naturally I refused to do any such thing.
Twice he exhorted me to confess, but in vain.
Then the executioner seized me and laid me on
the rack to torture me. But the rack proved to have
been made for bodies of a size different from mine,
so I had to scramble down again and stand and
wait while they altered it so that it could be used
for a dwarf. I had to listen to their obscenities and
foolish jests and their assurances that they were
going to make a fine tall fellow of me. Then I was
put back on the rack and they began to torment me
in the most horrible way. Despite the pain I did
not utter a sound but gazed scornfully at them as
they performed their despicable trade. The man
of law bent over me, trying to extract my secret
from me, but not a word passed my lips. I did not
betray her. I did not want her debasement to be
known.

Why did I behave thus? I do not know. But I preferred to endure the worst rather than reveal anything which might degrade her. I compressed my lips and let them plague me for the sake of that detestable woman. Why? Perhaps I liked suffering for her sake.

At last they had to give up. They loosened the ropes, swearing vilely all the while. I was taken to a dungeon and loaded with the chains which had been made that time when I gave communion to my oppressed people and which, therefore, now came in very useful. That was a less inhospitable prison than my present one. A couple of days later I was brought up again and went through the same treatment. But again it was all in vain. Nothing could make me speak. I still carry her secret in my heart.

After a time I was confronted by a kind of court of justice where I learned that I was accused of all manner of crimes, among others that of having caused the death of the Princess. I did not know that she was dead, but I am sure that on hearing it not a muscle of my face betrayed my emotion. She had died without ever awaking from her coma.

They asked me if I had anything to say in my defense. I did not deign to answer. Then came the verdict. For all my wicked deeds and as the cause of so many misfortunes, I was condemned to be welded to the wall in the darkest dungeon under the fortress and to remain there in chains for all eternity. I was a viper and the evil genius of his Most Princely Grace, and it was his expressed wish that I should be rendered harmless for all time.

I listened unmoved to the sentence. My ancient dwarf face showed only scorn and mockery and I noticed that the sight of it filled them with fear. I was taken away from the court and since then I have seen none of these despicable beings except Anselmo who is so puerile that he is beneath my contempt.

Viper!

It is true that I mixed the poison, but on whose orders? It is true that I was the death of Don Riccardo, but who was it wished his death? It is true that I scourged the Princess, but who begged and prayed me to do so?

Human beings are too feeble and exalted to shape their own destiny.

One might have thought that I should have been condemned to death for all these atrocious crimes, but only the heedless and those who do not know my noble lord can be surprised that this was not so. I knew him far too well ever to fear anything like that; nor has he really so much power over me.

Power over me! What does it matter if I sit here in the dungeon? What good does it do if they clap me in irons? I still belong to the castle just as much as before! To prove it they have even welded me to it! We are forged together, it and I! We cannot escape from each other, my master and I! If I am imprisoned, then he is imprisoned too! If I am linked to him, then he too is linked to me!

Here I am in my hole, living my obscure mole life, while he goes about in his fine handsome halls. But my life is also his, and his noble highly respectable life up there really belongs to me.

I⊤ HAS taken me several days to put this down. I can only write during the short time when a ray of sunlight from the narrow slit falls on the paper: then I must seize the opportunity. The ray moves along the dungeon floor for an hour, but I cannot follow it, owing to the chain which fastens me to the wall. I can only move a tiny bit. Therefore, it also took me a long time to read through what I had written. But that was an advantage, for thereby the distraction lasted that much longer.

I have nothing to do the rest of the day, and remain seated as before. By three o'clock it gets dark, and I have to spend the greater part of the time in complete darkness. Then the rats come out and creep around, their eyes shining. I see them at once for I too can see in the dark and, like them, I have become more and more of an underground creature. I hate those dirty ugly beasts and hunt them by sitting quite still until they come near enough for me to trample them to death. That is one of the few manifestations of vitality left to me. In the morning I order Anselmo to throw them away. I cannot think where they come from: it must be the door which does not shut properly.

Moisture drips down the wall and the cell has a musty smell which irritates me more than anything else, I think, for I am very sensitive to such things. The floor is of earth, hardened by the feet of those who have languished here. They cannot have been chained to the wall as I am, at least not all of them, for the whole floor seems to be like stone. At night I rest on a heap of straw, as she did. But it is not foul and stinking like hers, for I make Anselmo change it once a week. I am no penitent. I am a free man. I do not degrade myself.

Such is my existence in this dungeon. I sit here setting my jaw and thinking my thoughts about life and human beings as I have always done, and I do not change in the least.

If they think they can subdue me they are wrong!

I HAVE had some contact with the outer world, thanks to the good man who is my jailer. When he comes with my food he tells me in his guileless way of what has happened, adding lengthy commentaries of his own. He is very much interested in everything and likes to voice the speculations which have caused him such travail. In his mouth everything becomes utterly fatuous: above all he wonders what can be God's reasons for all that has happened. But my wider knowledge and experience help me to gain an approximate notion of what really took place, of all the circumstances attendant on the decline and death of the Princess and various other occurrences which followed my imprisonment. The Prince sat faithfully by her bed all day long watching her face become more and more transparent and what the court described as spiritualized. As though he had seen her himself, Anselmo maintained that she became as lovely as a madonna. I who really did see her knew how much truth there was in that. But I can quite believe that the Prince sat there and devoted himself entirely to the wife who was about to leave him. Perhaps he relived their youthful love. If so, he had to do it alone, for she was already far from all earthly ties. I know what he is like and undoubtedly he found something very moving in her unearthliness and remoteness. At the same time he must have been bewildered by her conversion, in which he had had no part, and probably wanted to call her back to life again. But she slipped through his hands, imperceptibly and without any explanations. Doubtless that increased his love; it generally seems to.

It was in such a mood that he had me jailed and tortured. He loved her because she was so unattainable and, because of that, he let me suffer. It does not surprise me, but then nothing surprises me.

Bernardo was there with some others, and saw her. The old master is said to have observed that her face was wonderful to look upon and that now he was beginning to understand it, and to comprehend why his portrait of her had been a failure. It is not all certain that it was a failure, though she no longer resembled it. I think he ought to have realized that and pondered on it.

Then the priests put in their appearance, running in and out, declaring her entry into the eternal life to be a beautiful and elevating sight. Her own confessor must also have been there, telling everybody who would listen that she was without sin. When she was very near the end, the archbishop gave her communion and the last rites with his own hands and the whole room was full of prelates and spiritual dignitaries in full canonicals. But she died all alone, without knowing that anybody was there.

After her death they found a dirty crumpled paper on which she had written that she wished to have her despicable body burned like that of the plague victims, and the ashes strewn on the street so that all might tread on them. These words, though undoubtedly they were sincerely meant, were looked upon as incoherent wanderings and nobody paid any heed to her last wishes. Instead, they took a middle course, embalmed her corpse and then placed it in a simple iron coffin which was borne unadorned through the streets to the princely crypt in the cathedral. The procession was as meager as was possible where a princess was concerned, and the commonest people walked very devoutly in it, the miserable starved wretches who still survived. Anselmo described this cortege through the plague-smitten city as something very moving and pathetic. It is quite possible that it was.

The people believed that now they knew everything about her and her last days. They took possession of her as their own rightful property, changing what they had heard according to their own fancy, as happens in such cases. Their imagination was stirred by the plain ugly coffin in the crypt among all the other magnificent princely coffins of silver and skillfully carved marble. Lying there, she seemed somehow to have become one of them. And her penances and scourgings, which the tiring wench had had time to relate to all and sundry, transformed her into one of the elect who, being an exalted personage despite her humiliation, had suffered more than all the others. Inasmuch as He was God's son, Jesus too suffered more than anybody else even though many others have been crucified, some head downward, and had been killed and martyrized far more painfully than He. By degrees she became a saintly being who had despised and denied this life to such an extent that she had tortured her body to death of her own accord. Thus the legend was going on quite unaffected by reality, and they continued to work at it until it corresponded to their desires. God knows if there were not miracles by the black ugly iron coffin which contained her remains. At least Anselmo believed that there were. He declared that a light shone about it at night. This is possible. The cathedral is closed at that time so nobody can authentically deny or affirm it, and when believers have the choice between that which is true and that which is not, they always choose that which is not. Lies are far rarer and more impressive than the truth, and so they prefer them.

When I heard all this I was obliged to tell myself that, quite unsuspectingly, I had been the creator of this saintly halo, or at least contributed largely to its sheen. And because of that, I was now manacled to the wall down here. Of course they knew nothing about that, and had they done so they certainly would have taken no interest in my martyrdom. Nor did I desire anything of that kind. But I was surprised that anyone so unholy as I should be instrumental in bringing about anything like that.

In due time, I do not quite remember when, Anselmo began to relate how Bernardo was painting a Madonna with the features of the Princess. The Prince and the whole court were very absorbed in the work and greatly pleased with it. The old master explained that he wanted to reproduce her innermost self and all that he had been able to apprehend only vaguely before he saw her on her deathbed. I do not know if he succeeded, not having seen the result but merely having heard it spoken of as an extraordinary masterpiece—however, they say the same of all his work. He took a long time over it but in the end he did finish it. His Holy Communion with Christ breaking bread for those around the table is still incomplete and will remain so, but he really did complete this picture. Maybe that kind of thing is easier. It has been hung in the cathedral at an altar on the left of the nave and Anselmo was full of childish admiration when he saw it. He described it in his simple way and said that everybody felt that such a madonna, such a gracious and celestial Mother of God had never been depicted before. Most entrancing of all was the enigmatic smile which hovered around her lips, which affected everyone as being something quite heavenly, inexplicable and full of divine mysticism. I understood that the artist had taken that smile from his earlier portrait, the one in which she resembled a whore.

It was not easy to get any notion of the picture from the foolish Anselmo's descriptions, but as far as I could understand, the master really had succeeded in creating something which must appeal to the devout. He himself can scarcely believe in the Mother of God, yet he had been able to impregnate her portrait with a sincere religious feeling and thereby fill the onlooker with pious emotion. Crowds came to the heavenly new Madonna and it was not long before they were kneeling before her with candles in their hands. There were more worshipers there than at any other altar, and so many tapers in the candlesticks before the portrait of the deceased Princess that their flames were the first thing one saw on entering the cathedral. The poor especially, all those who were unhappy and oppressed in these troublous times, assembled there to pray and seek consolation in their plight. She became their favorite Madonna, patiently listening to their troubles and sorrows and giving them help and solace, though as far as I know she never gave a thought to the poor. Thus Bernardo, with his great art, roused the deep and religious feelings of the people, just as I do.

While relating this, I cannot refrain from pondering over the strangeness of it all. Who could believe that this woman would hang in the cathedral, as a gentle consolatory Madonna, a shrine for the love and adoration of all the people? That she should reign pure and celestial in the light of innumerable candles dedicated to her purity and kindness? Her other portrait is in the palace, for the Prince had it framed and hung, though Maestro Bernardo is dissatisfied with it. That is the one in which she looks like a whore. And yet both pictures, despite their great dissimilarity, may speak the truth each in its own way; both show the same vague smile, which the worshipers in the cathedral think so heavenly.

Human beings like to see themselves reflected in clouded mirrors.

Since describing all this, that is to say everything that has happened from the time I was imprisoned, I find that I have nothing left to write about. Anselmo still comes here and tells me what is happening in the town and at the court, but there has been nothing very special. The plague subsided at last after having accounted for a large part of the population; it disappeared of its own accord as it had come, and cases became fewer and fewer until at last they ceased altogether. By degrees life resumed its old ways and, despite everything, the town became itself again. The peasants returned to their burned-out farms and built them up again, and slowly the land began to recover, though it was still impoverished. The war debts were tremendous and the state coffers empty. Therefore, as Anselmo explained to me, the people were weighed down with heavy taxation. But anyhow there was peace, as he expressed it, and something would always turn up. Then everything would be all right. "They are feeling cheerful now in the country," he said and his silly face glowed with satisfaction.

He entertains me with his perpetual chatter on all subjects and I listen to him, since I have no one else to talk to, though sometimes he can be very exhausting. The other day he came and said that the great debt to Venice at last had been paid and the land was free from this heavy burden. "Things are improving and better times are coming after the great trials, one can see it all over the place," he said. "They have even begun work on the campanile again, after all these years, and hope to have it ready before too long." I mention this though actually it is scarcely worth writing down.

Nothing very interesting happens nowadays.

I sit here in my dungeon after waiting for what seems like an eternity for the ray of sunlight, and now, when it has come, I have nothing to put on the paper which it illuminates. The pen lies idle in my hand, I cannot bring myself to use it.

Writing becomes more and more boring because my existence is so utterly uneventful.

Tomorrow the campanile is going to be consecrated, and its bells will ring for the first time. They are made partly of silver, the result of a collection among all the people. They believe that this will add to the beauty of the timbre.

The Prince and the whole court will of course be present.

THE CONSECRATION has taken place and Anselmo has had a great deal to tell which he heard from those who were present. He declares that it was a notable and unforgettable event, in which nearly the whole population shared. The Prince went on foot through the town at the head of his court, and the streets were bordered by people who wanted to see him and be present at the solemn moment which impended. He looked grave but erect and supple as of old, and obviously happy on this great day. He and his followers were clad in the most gorgeous habiliments. On reaching the piazza outside the cathedral, he entered the church and knelt first by the Princess' coffin and then before the altar with her picture, and all the others knelt there with him. Their devotions concluded, they went out again to the cathedral square and the bells in the campanile began to ring. They sounded so beautiful that everybody was deeply affected and listened in silence to the indescribable peal which seemed to come from heaven. It echoed over the town and all felt happier for having heard it. The people who were assembled on the square around the Prince thought that they had never experienced anything like this before. That is how Anselmo described it.

To his disappointment, he could not be present at the consecration as it occurred at the time when the prisoners were fed, but he had to content himself listening to the bells from here. When they began to toll he came scurrying to me and said that now it had begun. He was so upset that he had to open the door so that I too could hear. I think there were tears in the worthy man's eyes and he declared that no human ear had ever heard such bells before. In point of fact, they sounded much as most bells do, there was nothing special about them. I was glad when he shut the door again and left me in peace.

I sit here in my chains and the days go by and nothing ever happens. It is an empty joyless life, but I accept it without complaint. I await other times and they will surely come, for I am not destined to sit here for all eternity. I shall have an opportunity of continuing my chronicle by the light of day as before, and my services will be required again. If I know anything of my lord, he cannot spare his dwarf for long. I muse on this in my dungeon and am of good cheer. I reflect on the day when they will come and loosen my chains, because he has sent for me again.